The Present Tense
of Prinny Murphy

The Present Tense of Prinny Murphy

Jill MacLean

Fitzhenry & Whiteside

Published in Canada by Fitzhenry & Whiteside,
195 Allstate Parkway, Markham, Ontario L3R 4T8

Published in the United States by Fitzhenry & Whiteside,
311 Washington Street, Brighton, Massachusetts 02135

www.fitzhenry.ca   godwit@fitzhenry.ca

10 9 8 7 6 5 4 3 2 1

Library and Archives Canada Cataloguing in Publication

MacLean, Jill
The present tense of Prinny Murphy / Jill MacLean.
ISBN 978-1-55455-145-3
I. Title.
PS8575.L415P74 2009   jC813'.6   C2009-904304-1

**U.S. Publisher Cataloging-in-Publication Data
(Library of Congress Standards)**

McLean, Jill.
The present tense of Prinny Murphy / Jill McLean.
[232] p. :   cm.
Summary: Prinny is struggling with reading, bullying, an alcoholic mother, and
losing her best friend to the new girl at school. But a special book shows her
that life can be full of possibilities and poetry.
ISBN: 978-1-55455-145-3 (pbk.)
1. Bullying -- Juvenile fiction. 2. Schools -- Juvenile fiction. I. Title.
[Fic] dc22   PZ7.M454 2009

Fitzhenry & Whiteside acknowledges with thanks the Canada Council for the Arts, and
the Ontario Arts Council for their support of our publishing program. We acknowledge
the financial support of the Government of Canada through the Book Publishing Industry
Development Program (BPIDP) for our publishing activities.

Canada Council   Conseil des Arts
for the Arts   du Canada

Design by Fortunato Design Inc.
Cover Design by Duncan Campbell
Cover Images by Eric Begin and Christie Harkin

Printed in Canada

Acknowledgements

This book pays homage to Virginia Euwer Wolff's classic novel, *Make Lemonade*.

My deep appreciation to Martine Leavitt
for *Heck Superhero*
and
Kenneth Oppel for *Silverwing*

My warm thanks go out to:

Mary Jo Anderson, Sue MacLeod, and Barbara Markovits, for reading the manuscript and giving me their valuable insights.

Sue MacLeod for the title.

Dodie, Colin, Jessica, and Stuart MacLean for answering my many questions.

Faye Roberts for her help with boat names.

Jane Buss of the Writers' Federation of Nova Scotia for unfailing support.

Gail Winskill for her faith in Prinny.

Christie Harkin and Sonya Gilliss for all the work behind the scenes—with a special thank you to Kate Harkin for the beautiful cover picture.

Ann Featherstone, my editor, for her experience, her astute eye and—equally important—her sense of humor.

And lastly, all the many readers of *The Nine Lives of Travis Keating* who wanted to know what happened next....

For Dodie

ONE

mis·'step

You ever set out to do something mean, then have second—and third—thoughts?

I'm standing on Aunt Ida's doorstep, thought number four taking shape, my fingers wrapped around the handle of Ma's pink and brown suitcase. You could eat off Aunt Ida's doorstep.

I give a half-hearted rap on the door. Aunt Ida whips it open, as if she saw me coming. Not waiting for her to say *Hello, Prinny, how nice to see you*, because she never does, I edge the suitcase over the threshold.

"This here has more of Ma's clothes in it. You can—"

She grips me by the elbow and hauls me indoors. Then she knees the door shut, the latch snapping like a rat trap. "You can give Wilma the suitcase yourself. Past time she woke up. Banging on my door at four a.m. as if she lives here!"

Everything about Aunt Ida's pulled tight: skin over her cheekbones, hair in a bagel-shaped bun, but most of all her temper, vibrating like an anchor-line snagged in the tide.

My legs move down the hall as though I'm wearing rubber boots full of water. Aunt Ida blats away behind me. "Don't know why I get stuck with Wilma whenever she's too drunk to find her way back to Sebina's place."

Ma's in the parlor, laying on the couch, eyes shut. I wrinkle my nose. Stale smoke, stale booze, and stale Ma. Mascara gobs her lashes, plum lipstick smears the corners of her mouth. It's past understanding why my friend Travis Keating's ma, who by all accounts was decent, is dead, while my ma blunders on.

I'm standing beside her coffin, wearing a new green wool coat with a stand-up collar, and shiny leather boots. Ma's in a dress, a respectable navy-blue dress, her lipstick a soft shade of pink. I lean over, kiss her cold cheek, and place a single white rose on her folded hands....

I say loudly, "Hello, Ma."

She gives a little start, rubs her eyes, lifts her head, moans, and *thunks* it back on the pillow. "Prinny," she whispers. "How are you, darlin'?"

"I brought your summer clothes."

"Summer...? It's only April."

"You'll be needing them soon enough."

"I'll be home long before summer."

"Maybe. Maybe not."

She struggles to sit up. Her sweatshirt's stained and you can see she hasn't bothered with a bra. "How's your da?" she says.

"He's fine. I cooks for him every day. He likes that."

"Don't you go thinking you can take my place!"

"You got no place anymore, Ma. Da kicked you out, remember? The night you fired a beer bottle at the TV."

"Sebina's coming after lunch to take me back to St. Fabien. I'll clean myself up and be home tomorrow."

"Sure—if the liquor store's shut, and every club from here to Blandings."

She flinches. Like a rogue wave, guilt washes over me. But not so deep that I keep my mouth shut. "Da told you the only way you can come home is if you quit drinking."

"I'm off the booze. I swear I am."

"Promises are the cheapest deal in town."

"You're mean as a weasel!"

"Who made me that way?"

Her eyes fill. "How come everything's always my fault?"

Is there anything worse than Ma with a hangover and tears dripping off her chin? "I never said that… I gotta go. We eats dinner at noon."

She swipes at her eyes, leaving a streak of mascara across her cheek. "I'll be home first thing tomorrow, you wait and see."

"I'm done waiting for you."

Right on top of the clothes in the suitcase is my latest report card. On it, Mrs. Dooks wrote, *Prinny appears to be paying more attention this term*. Ma'll get the message. For all the rum and beer she's downed, she's not dumb.

All this time Aunt Ida hasn't said a word. I slide past her, not looking her in the eye. Her and Ma are sisters, same mother, same father, grew up in the same house—and one's a shark and the other's a jellyfish. Aunt Sebina is their sister, too. She's as kind as anyone can be. Ma's been living with her and Uncle Ralph for the last five months.

If I had a sister, would she be like Aunt Sebina? Would she bring Ma a glass of water, wash her face, tell her she loves her?

If I had a sister, I bet I'd be a nicer person.

Aunt Ida puts the flat of her hand in the small of my back and shoves me down the hall. "In my day, you weren't rude to your elders."

I collapse like a farting balloon. It's one thing to sass Ma; over the last few months I've gained the upper hand with her. But Aunt Ida? Her wrath's on a par with God's.

"Sorry."

"Honor thy father and thy mother, that's what we were taught. And that's what we did, or out came the belt."

So if you believe in the commandments, Aunt Ida, how come you never go to church? For an awful moment I think I've said this out loud, and my knees quiver like I'm the jellyfish. Thin-lipped, she adds, "When you're in my house, mind your manners. You better wait for your uncle—he'll drive you home."

"Da's at the wharf."

"Then why didn't *he* bring the suitcase?"

"Da? You only have to mention Ma and he acts like a dog that's just been walloped."

"Your mother needs you, Prinny," Aunt Ida says. And I realize she's taken herself by surprise as much as me.

I lunge for the door and I'm down the steps before the demon on my tongue can scream, "What about me? Maybe I needs something, too—a mother I can depend on!"

The door slams. Aunt Ida back in character. The road wavers because I'm near to crying. I set off to walk to the wharf, my old brown boots pinching my toes.

Two

′res·cu·er

The gray shingles on Abe Murphy's barn are cracked and split; but the latch on the door is new and the hinges freshly oiled. I always try and arrive before Travis, in hopes that my favorite daydream will become reality: *me sitting on a bale of straw, the sun on my hair. Ghost, the white cat, curled in my arms, gazing at me adoringly. "Prinny," Travis will say as he comes in the barn door, "you've tamed Ghost! How did you do that? You're some smart."*

I'm late today. So when I push the door open, Travis is the one sitting on the bale of straw, the sun's gone behind a cloud, and Rocky, the big gray cat, is perched on his knees.

The cow turns her head, wisps of hay sticking out of her rubbery pink lips. The hens go *cluck-urrk, cluck-urrk*. As I walk closer, Travis keeps stroking the cat, talking to him in a low voice. Rocky stays put. I crouch down so as not to frighten him.

"He's much tamer than he used to be," I say.

"Yeah…wish Ghost would take a lesson from him."

12

"It's not that long since you brought them here, Travis—saved them from starving to death at Gulley Cove."

"You helped. Remember loaning me snowshoes after the blizzard so I could go out there to feed them?"

"Then you asked Da if I could have the two kittens for my birthday. How brave was that?"

He ducks his head. "Now all we have to do is find homes for these guys."

Four of the cats live in Abe's barn: Rocky, Patches, Ghost, and Cloud. They were too wild to give to anyone, and they couldn't stay at Gulley Cove—nothing there but an old wharf and some beat-up fish shacks. Once a week Travis and I come to the barn and work on taming the cats. Abe's real good to them, feeding them every day and giving them shots of milk from the cow.

"Patches is doing okay," I say, sitting down next to him and rubbing Rocky's chin. "My Aunt Sebina said she might want a cat—she liked the sound of Patches. There's mice in their shed."

"That's where your mother's staying, isn't it?"

I smirk. "Not in the shed. Too bad—might knock some sense in her. Have you seen Ghost today?"

"Your mother will straighten out, Prinny."

"When fish grow feathers."

Travis gives me one of his looks; he likes people to get along. "You want her to come home—you just won't admit it."

"Ma's not a can of worms, she's a whole truck-load. And no, I don't want her home!"

I want her back at Aunt Sebina's; she'll have left Aunt Ida's by now to go there.

"You're so stubborn!"

"I asked if you've seen Ghost."

Travis sighs. "He's hiding somewhere—I haven't seen him for a couple of weeks. Don't suppose we'll ever find a home for him."

"Not unless someone wants an invisible cat."

It still amazes me how Travis and me can have a fight and stay friends.

Travis has dark curly hair and straight teeth, and although he's still the shortest guy in our grade, he's grown a full inch since January. I'm tall for a girl, but one of these days the top of his head will rise above my chin.

"I figure Abe will move Cloud into the house soon," he says, cheering up. "Cloud's the only one who'll look him in the eye."

"Two down, two to go...the barrens were right pretty today."

Out behind Ratchet, where we both live, the barrens stretch for miles, granite and bog, juniper,

14

crowberry, and bakeapple. Ratchet, I might as well tell you straight up, is the end of the road. And in northern Newfoundland, that's not a word of a lie.

After a while, Cloud stalks toward us. He knows the hens are too big for him to tackle, so he ignores them. Allowing me to pat him, he arches his back and purrs. Then Patches pounces on him from behind the straw and they're into it.

Travis says, "So what did you do all weekend?"

The thing is, he really wants to know. I ramble on about the latest nature show on TV. Then I tell him about the caribou tracks I saw in the snow on Friday, and pass him two of the chocolate drop cookies I baked last night. I don't tell him about going to Aunt Ida's with Ma's suitcase; I'd get another of his looks.

The cookies are right tasty.

Sunlight has hitched itself to little specks of dust in the air. When the cow shifts in her stall, the straw rustles. I smile at Travis. He smiles back. Then Cloud butts my hand, impatient to have his head scratched.

As we walk home along the road, Travis tells me how the NHL semi-finals are going. He joined our local hockey team last fall and rescued them from their worst slump in years. Six cats, two kittens, and one hockey team. Not bad.

After he says goodbye at the bottom of his drive-way, I run up the street to my place.

I'm not one bit worried Ma might have turned up while I was gone.

THREE

pre·mo·ʹni·tion

A four-syllable word, right, and impossible to tell what it means, even after you subtract the *pre-* and the *-tion*. Happens I do know because it was in the paragraph I had to read out loud last week and I called it *pre·moan·ʹi·shun*. By the time Mrs. Dooks was finished with me, no way I'd forget how to spell premonition, how to pronounce it, or what it means.

When I climb out of bed Monday morning, I don't have the foggiest notion of what's to come.

I'm up half an hour early so I can wash my hair. No amount of washing changes it from dead-leaf brown, but I likes—like—the way it fans out when I use Ma's old hairdryer.

Did you notice how I changed *likes* to *like*? Hanging around with Travis is teaching me to talk different. I'm cutting out a lot of stuff, starting with *ain't* and *arse*, and, when I remembers, that *s* on the end of the first person singular present tense.

Mostly I remember. Slip-ups can happen when things get tense, which is less often now Ma's moved out.

Travis's ma taught English in grade eight before she got sick and died. Travis never says *ain't*.

By eight o'clock I'm gathering up my books, my clean hair swinging in a ponytail. The menu for supper is printed neatly on a notepad on the kitchen counter; I'm into cooking proper meals since Ma left. The break-fast dishes are done, a load of Da's overalls and T-shirts are dancing a jig on the clothesline, my cats are fed, and the litter scooped. All this makes me feel like I got a hold on the day.

Only downside in view is remedial reading this afternoon with Mrs. Dooks.

I step outdoors. The sun's shining and you can smell spring even though dirty slush edges the roads and snow lies deep in the hollows. The sea's sparkling like Aunt Sebina's earrings, the ones she bought at Le Bijou. You might as well know right from the get-go that the other thing I love, aside from the barrens, is the sea. Both of them do away with the emptiness inside me.

No point waiting around for a definition of this emptiness. Can't say I understand it myself. When I was little, I called it "the gap" until I found out this was the name for a chain of fancy stores selling the kind of clothes we can't afford. Although I never found another name, it doesn't seem so important now that Travis is my friend.

The school bus pulls up at the end of our lane.

"Hi, Mr. Murphy," I say. He's our regular driver. Then I say, "Hi, Travis."

"Hi, Prinny. I forgot to ask yesterday how your cats are doing."

"Seven-thirty this morning Tansy found Da's twine for mending nets. Rogue got all tangled up in it while Tansy sat back looking innocent as butter."

He starts telling me about the dead voles his cat Felix has been lining up on the front step every morning. Then Hector Baldwin climbs on the bus, and we say hi again. You're either a Murphy or a Baldwin if you're from Ratchet.

Mr. Murphy says, "We have a new kid to pick up today. I'm told her name's Lace Hadden and that she'll be staying here with her grandparents until school's over. She lives near Halifax."

Hector grunts. He's not much for talking.

Travis says, "Why did she come to Ratchet?"

"You'll have to ask her," Mr. Murphy says, levering the door shut before he drives up the road.

We look at each other. It's not even a year since Travis moved here with his dad from St. John's, and now here's another new kid in Ratchet. I've never been off Newfoundland, let alone to Halifax. All of a sudden I have the strong urge to chew on the end of my ponytail, a habit Aunt Ida says is immature, unattractive, and gives me split ends.

"Lace," I say, "what kind of a name's that?"

Even to myself, I sound mingy. Prinny's not much of a name either, not short for Priscilla or Primrose, and not helped any by my second name, which is Bethiah after Da's great-grandmother who lived in Ballyshannon. I say quickly, "It'll be fun to have a girl my age in Ratchet."

Soon as I say that, little white-hot needles skitter around inside me. Not in a million years would I tell Travis about them; there's plenty of stuff I don't tell him, him being a guy and all. But maybe, just maybe, Lace will become my girlfriend, someone I can tell anything to. Someone who'll fill the emptiness.

If she's from Halifax, she probably wears clothes from that store. The Gap. So I guess with her I'd have to call the gap "loneliness" even though I've always known lonely isn't a large enough word.

A girl's standing by the side of the road outside the last house in Ratchet. Mr. Murphy stops the bus. "Good morning, Lace."

She climbs aboard. I shrink back in my seat. She's beautiful as a Barbie doll. Blond curls, dark blue eyes with long lashes, and flushed cheeks. Her snow jacket has white fur on the hood. Her boots are real leather.

Mr. Murphy says, smiling at her, "These kids' names are Prinny, Travis, and Hector—all from

Ratchet and all in the same grade as you."

So she's pretty—so what? My hair's clean, Travis is my friend, and so is Hector in his own way. I swallow hard. Patting the seat beside me, I smile at her. "You can sit here if you like."

Her eyes dart from my frayed backpack and the worn cuffs of my jacket down to my boots, which weren't much to start with. She's not sneering. Not quite.

Way back in kindergarten I learned never to cry on the bus.

"Hi, Lace," Travis says. His voice sounds kind of funny, as if the opposing hockey team just scored a goal and he didn't see it coming. "I hope you'll like living here."

She looks at him, a look that would freeze Long Pond clear to the bottom. "I'm only staying in Ratchet two months," she says. "I didn't want to come and I can't wait to leave."

Even though I don't like her talking to Travis that way, I try one more time. "Lace is a nice name. I used to have a yellow blouse with lace on the collar."

She turns that icy look on me. "My name's spelled L-a-i-c-e." Then she walks past all three of us, sitting down near the back where the big kids sit.

Mr. Murphy jams the bus in gear and starts out across the barrens toward Fiddlers Cove, the next place west. Hector stares out the window. Travis stares at the back of Mr. Murphy's head. I stare at Travis.

Usually you can't shut Travis up on the bus.

First stop at Fiddlers Cove is to pick up Hud Quinn. Hud's tall and skinny, his hair sleek as a wet seal. He's my first cousin, not that I go around boasting about that. Back in the fall, if it hadn't been for Travis, Hud would have thrown Ghost—locked in a cat cage—into the sea. Instead it was Hud who ended up in the sea. One more reason why I think Travis is special.

One more reason why Hud hates Travis.

When Hud sees Laice, he stops in his tracks. "Little kids sit near the front of the bus."

Mr. Murphy sighs. "Go sit down, Hud, and leave her alone."

"Yeah, yeah," Hud says and shambles down the aisle.

Other kids get on at the cove and Long Bight, and each time Mr. Murphy says, "The new girl's name is Laice, say hello to her." Some do and some don't. Either way, Laice keeps her mouth shut.

In our home room my seat's near the back, one row over and three seats behind Travis, who's sitting next to Laice. He spends the first two periods gaping at her; he flubs the algebra problem he has to put on the board. All the other boys are gawking, too. Finally the bell rings for recess.

What I generally do at recess is walk a lot, starting from the door where we're let out and traveling along the fence, back and forth, avoiding the boys' side where they're playing ball-hockey (Travis's grade) or lighting up (Hud's grade), and keeping my eyes peeled for the Shrikes, who pick on me a fair bit because of my ma. The fence is wire mesh, so the wind scarcely knows it's there, the sky's free no matter where you are, and in my mind I'm stalking caribou on the barrens, every nerve alert, and that way I stay out of trouble and the fifteen minutes usually go pretty fast.

Today's got a different feel. Laice is standing all alone near the basketball hoop, the boys loosely circling her, the girls clumped to one side. Then the Shrikes saunter out the door, one by one.

Never make eye contact with the Shrikes.

They see Laice right away, changing direction as though she's a magnet. There's Melanie Corkum, call-me-Mel-or-I'll-pound-your-face-in, who's repeating her year and whose boobs make the boys cross-eyed; Sigrid Sugden, whose jeans are so tight she likely pulls them on damp and puts the hair dryer to them; and Tate Cody, the smallest and scariest because you never know what she's going to do next.

They're all in my grade. Lucky me.

Okay, so you're wondering why I call them the Shrikes. One day last spring, out on the barrens, three gray birds landed on an old spruce tree right in front of me. I never saw the likes of them before, so my next trip to the school library I went through the bird book until I found their picture.

Because I couldn't read the print—too many big words—I screwed up my courage and asked the librarian to read it for me. Upshot is, the birds are called shrikes. Migrating north, they were. They kill smaller birds, tearing them apart to eat them. Well, that's nature, happens all the time. But shrikes go one step farther. Sometimes they shove the bird on a thorn, just leave it hanging there until they get hungry enough to eat it.

The bird's dead. But still.

Mel says loudly, "What have we got here?"

Laice looks up at her—did I mention Laice is petite? There's nothing petite in the way she's eyeing Mel though. I should scream, *Don't do that! Run!*

Laice says in a voice like ice crystals, "My name is Laice Hadden. I live near Halifax. I'll only be here until the end of term."

The boys move a little closer. So do I. I'm fingering the bone I keep in my pocket, wing bone of a bird, hollow like a flute, which I like to think is why birds sing so sweet.

Mel depends on brute size, not being the sharpest axe in the woodpile. As she fumbles for an insult gross enough for a come-from-away who dared talk back to her, Sigrid flips the fur on Laice's hood. "A little bunny rabbit died just so you can wear this."

"You don't know much about fur, do you?" Laice says, her chin tilted. But I'm watching her hands, how her knucklebones jut through the skin. Someone should've warned her. I should have.

Tate says in her raspy voice, "You planning on being a model when you grow up?"

"Actually, an astrophysicist," Laice says.

"Well, la-di-da," Tate says, her eyes like nail holes.

The teacher on yard duty is over where the boys hang out. Even though Laice was mean to me on the bus, and meaner still to Travis, I could run and get him. Before anything happens. But if I do, I'll miss what does happen. Besides, if the Shrikes are picking on Laice, they're leaving me alone.

Mel surges forward, grabs Laice by the shoulders, and lifts her off her feet, shaking her so her teeth clack together and her hood flaps up and down. "We run this show," Mel says. "The three of us. You got that?"

Laice's cheeks are as white as the fur on her hood. She's afraid, which changes her from a Barbie doll to a real person, a person I gotta help. But I can't locate my backbone.

Laice doesn't wait for me—she jabs at Mel with the toe of her fancy boot. I squawk in dismay. Attack the Shrikes? Worth your life to do that.

Next thing you know, Travis skids to a halt in front of Mel. "Put her down!"

Mel hoists Laice higher. "Make me."

Travis sinks his fist in the pudge of Mel's belly because she's left it wide open, then kicks her hard on the kneecap.

Mel drops Laice and hunches over, bellowing like a bull moose. Sigrid's mouth is hanging open, while Tate looks like she could stick a knife between Travis's ribs and happily watch the blood flow. She says, real quiet, "You'll wish you hadn't done that."

"Yeah, yeah," Travis says.

Cole, Buck, and Stevie, all members of the St. Fabien Furies hockey team, form a defensive line in front of him and Laice. Hector, who usually only grunts, hollers, "Mr. Marsden! Help! Mr. Marsden!"

I'm just standing there. I haven't done anything.

Mr. Marsden comes on the run. Travis is patting Laice on the shoulder; he's a whole inch taller than she is. Although she's still white about the gills, she's gazing at him like he's Superman. I edge farther away. The other thing I learned in kindergarten was never to cry in the schoolyard.

"What's the problem, Mel?" Mr. Marsden huffs.

"Who hurt you?"

The kids crowd around, everyone jabbering their version of what happened. Travis waits until things quiet down. "These three girls were bullying Laice."

"That's right," I whisper, "they were." But nobody hears me because they're all gabbing again.

Tate snarls, "We were not—we were just telling her we like her jacket."

The bell shrills for the end of recess. Looking flat-out relieved, Mr. Marsden says, "Line up, boys and girls, line up." Then he stands there while we shuffle into place.

I sit next to Hector in the cafeteria at noon because Travis is sitting with Laice on the other side of the room. My belly aches as if I'm the one got punched. Hector's chubby and hates gym, but he knows how to make beautiful birdhouses out of wood and he owns Blackie, who's the mother of my two cats. I chew my bologna sandwich on whole wheat with iceberg lettuce.

"Hector," I say, "I'm real scared of Mel."

"Me, too."

"At least you shouted for help."

"I didn't punch her. Not like Travis. I'm bigger than Travis."

There doesn't seem much left to say after that.

Four

do·′mes·tic

The day's not over yet—I still have to face remedial reading. Question: define remedial reading. Answer: on Friday, Mrs. Dooks gives me an easy-read book to work on over the weekend, then Monday afternoon in study period she sits me down at the back of the room and I read aloud to her and the kids snigger and she does a lot of heavy sighing and the print's big but I'm sweating so hard the letters thrash around like mackerel in a bucket.

Today Laice will be listening to me read; this morning it didn't take any of us long to realize she's ahead of us in English and French. To top it off, the books are boring—about two kids who have perfect parents and a perfect house, and who solve a different mystery in each book with the help of their perfect dog Ben. I may not read so good, but the clues hit you like a two-by-four to the forehead.

You wouldn't think, after all this, that I'd still like words. But I do, providing I can hear them and stash them in my brain.

Anyways, I'm in a state by two-thirty. But as I lurch along, line by line, sounding out the-new-man-on-the-street-who-keeps-his-blinds-drawn-all-day-and-the-only-lights-at-night-come-from-the-base-ment, I notice something's missing. No sighs. No sarcastic comments. Mrs. Dooks is scarcely paying attention.

She's staring off into space instead. If she wasn't Mrs. Dooks, I'd say she looked sad.

What's there for Mrs. Dooks to feel sad about? When Mr. Dooks died four years ago, most everyone at Baldwin's Store was of the opinion she was better off without him.

The bell rings. I snap the book shut. Mrs. Dooks says absently, "Not as bad as usual, Prinny."

Normally this would set me up for the rest of the day. But on the bus Travis and Laice sit together, her by the window, him on the aisle, and they talk the whole way home. After a few of the kids get off in Long Bight, I move to the back so I don't have to listen. I can still see them, though. Blond head and dark head close together. Shoulders touching.

If I'd been the one to punch Mel—if I'd been the hero— Laice would be talking to me, not him.

At home I roll out the pastry I made yesterday, fit it into the blue-flowered pie plate Ma made in her ceramic phase, and dump in a Mason jar of moose meat. All Ma's phases are scattered around the kitchen. A stained-glass seagull, wall-eyed, hanging in the window. A crocheted dishcloth on the sink tray. Snowmen made out of sea urchins, candles plastered with winkles.

Phases or crazes? She'd throw herself into a project, get bored, and move on to the next; or else she'd start drinking. She never had a sitting-still-in-one-place phase. She sure never had a why-don't-I-devote-all-my-attention-to-my-only-daughter phase. And will you tell me why I'm standing here thinking about Ma when I got better things to do?

The pie goes in the oven, then I peel potatoes, turnip, and carrots, put them on to boil, and add chopped cabbage. Fifteen minutes later, the porch door bangs shut. I line up the cutlery on the place mats. Da comes into the kitchen and heads straight for the sink, where he opens the taps full blast and splashes water over his face, his hands, the counter, and the floor.

"When's dinner?" he says.

"It'll be ready in five minutes."

"Better change my shirt. Got grease on it."

He must have been at Dave Baldwin's garage, helping out. When he squeezes past the table, his overalls catch on a place mat. The knife and fork go flying.

"It's okay, Da," I say. "I'll pick them up."

Da's fingers work small. But the rest of him walks the house like it's a boat dumped high and dry by the tide. For Da, the only real kind of floor is the ocean. He was a fisherman from way back, but the moratorium—fancy word for the government closing down the cod fishery, which they did before I was born—ended all that. He still goes out lobster season, jigs his five cod a day, and sometimes gets a berth on a shrimp boat. But it's nowheres near year-round. Gives him too much time to think about Ma, that's how I look at it.

I put out a clean knife and fork, drain the vegetables, and tip them into a bowl. The pie crust is brown and flaky, just like it's supposed to be. Da shovels his food down, something Ma used to get antsy about. Then he leans back.

"That was some good."

"There's more pie."

"Don't mind if I do." He helps himself. "Lobstering starts in three and a half weeks."

"Can I come out with you on weekends?"

"Don't see why not."

How it goes is, I gaff the lines while Da pulls the pots over the gunwales of *Wilma Marie* with the winch. We empty them, I rebait them, then he tips them back into the sea, the two of us working together like strands of a rope.

Dessert is leftover gingerbread with canned apple-sauce. Da buries his face in the local paper while he drinks his tea. I wish he'd talk to me instead, but I don't know how to tell him this and I don't know what we'd talk about. Ma's out as a subject of conversation. So are the Shrikes, Mrs. Dooks, and my latest report card. Because reading's such a big problem, my marks wobble between C- and F. F scares the pants off me. What if I fail while Travis moves up to the next grade?

So far my good memory has saved me, along with math, B + to A-, hauling my average up sufficient that I've squeaked through.

"A new girl was on the bus today," I say.

"Mattie and Starald's granddaughter. Pretty as a picture, they were saying at the store."

Da's never told me I'm pretty. Half the time I'm not sure he even sees me. "What color are my eyes, Da?"

The paper stays where it is. "Brown. You need me to tell you that?"

"Guess not." I get up and start clearing the dishes. Da knows I don't do so good at school, but he doesn't know why; he made sure he was up to his elbows in the engine of Abe Murphy's half-ton the evening of the last parent-teacher interviews, and before that, the job was supposed to be Ma's. "Rogue fell into the washer Saturday," I say. "Suds from his whiskers to his tail."

"Yeah? Fisheries is planning to announce new quotas for hake and perch—I'd like to get them fellas in Ottawa out in a dory."

I just ate a plateful of dinner. No call to feel empty.

For the last few months I've been going over to Travis's place every Tuesday after school for a cooking lesson with Rayleen Murphy, their housekeeper. Travis likes hanging around the kitchen watching us; so although he sits next to Laice on the afternoon bus today, I try not to mind too much. When the bus stops to let Laice off, she and Travis both stand up. Instead of sitting down again once Laice is on her way up the aisle, Travis follows her.

I blurt, "Today's the day I goes to your place, Travis."

He stops like he's been whacked on the head. "Rayleen'll be there," he mutters and stumbles down the steps after Laice.

Hector's staring out the window. For once I'm glad he's not a talker.

So when I arrive at Travis's, there's only Rayleen and me. She was none too friendly last fall because Ma's a Quinn from Fiddlers Cove, which in Ratchet means you're a deadbeat; but she came around when Travis and me became friends. Today we make pork patties and miracle cake. I get to take two slices home, then I have to hustle frying sausages and hash for Da.

At supper, I push my food around with my fork and can't come up with anything to say. Not that he notices. Same thing happens the next evening (fish chowder and *toutons* with molasses). Finally I say, "Will you drive me to the rink, Da? There's a playoff game at 7:30."

"You got chores?"

"Dishes won't take long. I already did my homework." I even did some extra reading. Now that Ma's gone, the house is clean and orderly, with space for me and my homework.

I whip through the dishes, then put on a heavy sweater, slinging Travis's old red hockey jacket over it—the one from before he moved to Ratchet that says St. John's Jets on the sleeve with his name in big letters underneath. Travis can score goals as easy as Clarry Murphy pulls quarters from his ears. If the St. Fabien Furies win tonight, they'll be in the finals on Saturday. So even though his jacket's too small for me, it makes me feel good inside.

I sit by myself on the bleachers overlooking center ice. Laice comes into the arena with her grandparents, who go upstairs to the heated room. She walks my way. She's wearing fancy tie-up boots and a fake fur vest over a pink mohair sweater. When she's level with me, she stops, staring at Travis's name embroidered on my sleeve. "Where did you get that jacket?"

"You related to my Aunt Ida? You sure sound like her."

"Related to you? No, thank you."

I give her look for look. "Travis gave me the jacket."

"At the next game, I'll be the one wearing it."

"No, you won't—Travis is my friend."

"Travis is my *boy*friend. Besides, it'll fit me."

Right away, I feel gawky as a moose calf. "Travis won't make me give it back!"

"He'll do whatever I ask. You might as well give it to me now, because I know he'd want me to have it."

"Then he can tell me so himself."

"He will—you're such a loser!" The heels of her boots tapping on the concrete, she heads for the far end of the rink where Travis is doing drills. She waves, he raises his stick in salute, then she smiles at him as though he's the only guy on the ice.

I want to go home. But I can't. Da's playing poker with his buddies and won't be back for another hour and a half. I head for the girls' washroom, concrete-block walls with orange paint that must have been on sale because who else would buy it. I hang around until I think the game's started, then I come back out.

Hud's in the corridor, his back to me, his hockey bag on the floor behind him. He's holding a skate over his head, a little kid's skate. Damon Sugden, who's in Novice, is jumping up and down, trying to reach the skate; his hair's sweaty, but it's not sweat that's running down his cheeks.

"Gimme my skate!"

"Say please."

"Please, Hud…"

Damon makes another leap for the skate. Hud swings it out of reach. "A loonie and it's yours," he says.

"A loonie? A whole dollar? I'll give you my bubble-gum."

"That's not worth a loonie."

"I don't have any money." A tear drips from Damon's chin. "My mom's waiting outside—she'll be mad if I'm late."

"Scared of your mama? Awww."

As I start sneaking up behind them, Damon grabs at Hud's sleeve. Hud knees him. Damon thuds into the wall. Very quietly, I unzip Hud's bag. Hockey gear smells worse than old bait.

Hud turns his head. "Hey! What're you doing?"

I dangle his jock strap in the air. "Give Damon his skate—or I'll hang this from the mirror in the girls' washroom."

He makes a lunge for it. Damon seizes his skate, jerking it away from Hud, who's glaring at me as if he'd like to hang me from the water pipes. Damon plus his gear disappear around the corner.

Mel, just by looking at me, can buckle my backbone. But for some reason I've never been that scared of Hud. His da, now, that's different. From Monday to Sunday, you don't want to tangle with my uncle Doyle.

I toss the jock strap at Hud. "Damon's dad broke his leg a few days ago—he's off work. Where's Damon going to get a loonie?"

"I was only kidding."

"Kid someone your own size."

"Good thing you're a girl," he sneers. "I don't pick on girls, not worth the effort."

"Our brains are bigger. That's why you leave us alone," I say, turn my back, and stroll back to the bleachers. Hud has a sister whose name is Fleur; she's somewhere between three and four. I bet he picks on her.

The game's already started. The St. Christopher goalie is a big guy who makes some great saves. Travis is brilliant, though—so fast you can scarcely keep track of him, so accurate that the Furies are up by four goals at the start of the third period. Then Travis shoots, the goalie deflects the puck to one of his own defense players, Stevie checks him, steals the puck, and flips it back to Travis, who shoots again. The puck slides, neat as can be, into the back of the net. Travis circles away from the goal post, raising his stick high. He sees me watching—yelling, actually—and gives me a big grin.

It's just like old times. I grin back, and the world's okay again.

FIVE

'dig·i·tal

Seems like recess comes around same way as the tides.

I'm walking up and down the fence, minding my own business, trying not to notice how Laice has cozied up to a couple of girls from St. Fabien, which is the only town of any size around here; it's about fifteen kilometers from Ratchet. The schools, the mall, the medical clinic where Travis's dad works as a doctor, they're all in St. Fabien. Joan Bidson is the mayor's daughter; Nicole's dad is a lawyer. Normally those girls don't give us outport kids the time of day.

All of a sudden Mel plants herself in front of me. "Guess what?" she says. "Your ma barfed all over the front steps of Tony's Pizza last night. Then she laid down on them, snoring like a foghorn. Tony and his brother had to haul her off the steps so they could hose them down."

Sigrid is sniggering, and other kids gather, hoping for a bit of excitement. Laice says something to Joan, who laughs.

"Why are you bothering to tell me?" I say. To be honest, I kind of squeak it.

"Thought you'd be interested, seeing as how she's your ma."

I say in a rush, "She don't live with us anymore. Hasn't for months. So why would I be interested?"

My knees feel like they're not connected to my ankles. Worse, it's like I'm betraying Ma. Mel towers over me. "Bet you'd like to know where she spends the nights."

The squeak goes one pitch higher. "That's her business."

Tate says, "Prinny's right, Mel. Her mother's moved out. No skin off Prinny's butt what she does with her time."

Mel's gaping at her, and so am I. Tate gives the sudden smile that shows what she could be like if she tried. "To prove there's no hard feelings, Prinny, why don't you drop over to Sigrid's place after school tomorrow? We'll watch a video, play a bit of music…okay?"

Is my brain out of whack? Tate Cody, smiling at me? I say uncertainly, "You're kidding, right?"

"Nope. It'd be fun."

"I cooks dinner for Da after school."

Tate's laugh has an edge like a filleting knife. "Men just look helpless—he can get his own supper. C'mon, give us the chance to say we're sorry."

Mel's scowling as if Tate's lost her mind. So is Sigrid. But Tate's the boss; they'll go along with whatever she says.

Just imagine if the Shrikes turned friendly, even for a few days. Not likely it would last much longer than that. But any way you look at it, a break's a break.

"Okay," I say over the thumping in my chest.

"Great," says Tate, turning away and directing the same smile at Sigrid and Mel. "If we sneak over by the school bus, we got time for a smoke before the bell rings."

I'm left staring at their backsides. Joan sneers, "The video's a new release—The Fiddlers Cove Chainsaw Massacre. You're the first victim."

Is Joan right? I put a lot of faith in smiles though, and Tate's was the genuine article. It must be true: for now, she's easing up on me because Ma's moved out.

If I turn her down, she'll really have it in for me.

Friday morning I tell Da I'm stopping off in Fiddlers Cove after school and I'll leave leftovers in the fridge. I hardly ever skive off because he pays me for cooking and cleaning; I'm saving the money for vet bills.

The word must have gotten out about Tate's invitation. On the bus, soon as I get on, Travis says, "Don't you go to Sigrid's, Prinny. It's asking for trouble."

"After ignoring me all week, you're telling me what to do?"

"Stay away from those three—they're poison."

"Alls we're going to do is watch a video."

"If you believe that, you're not just naïve, you're plain stupid!"

"You quoting Laice?"

"Leave Laice out of this," he says, as Hector climbs aboard. "Did you tell your father where you're going?"

"I'm not five years old!"

Hector takes one look at us and sits two seats back. Travis says, "If you're not home by dark, I'm going after you."

I get this warm feeling because he's looking out for me, but I'm mad enough to slam a book on his head. "Laice won't like that."

As the bus pulls up by her driveway, Travis has kind of a desperate look on his face. But when Laice gets on, he smiles at her, patting the seat beside him, and I know I've been forgotten.

By the time the bus approaches Fiddlers Cove that afternoon, I'm a mess of nerves. The Shrikes have been around a long time and they've never been known for being nice. But Mel got off in Long Bight, so there's only two of them to deal with, and there won't be any audience at Sigrid's; they play to the audience, them three.

When I step off the bus, I don't even look at Travis. Mr. Murphy says, "See you, Prinny."

I definitely hope so.

Sigrid's bungalow has tired-looking curtains at the windows. The yard's full of weeds. She turns the key in the lock. "My parents are in Corner Brook for the weekend, but my brother Lorne will be home later. Once the bars close."

Tate says, "We rented *Carrie* and *The Ring*. Which do you want to watch first, Prinny?"

"I can only watch the one. Told Da I'd be home by dark." Which is an outright lie.

"Let's go with *Carrie*, then—it's a classic. Want a Cherry Coke?"

Sigrid says, "I'll microwave the popcorn."

"How come Mel couldn't be here?" I ask.

"Her dad wanted her home," Tate says, handing me the video. "Set this up for us, okay?"

Mel's father is the same size as Da, but mean where Da's mild. Hog knuckles for hands. Almost enough to make you sorry for her.

I turn on the TV and DVD player and put the disc in. The credits start with the first scene—girls playing on a volleyball court—so I push Pause. The popcorn exploding in the microwave sounds like a war's going on. What makes my skin crawl is how the house reminds me of our house when Ma used to live there; the living room looks like there was a party last weekend that no one got around to cleaning up yet. *Unkempt* was on our dictionary list last week. Leave out the *m* and you've got *unkept*, no one caring enough to keep the place clean and tidy. I drop the remote on the coffee table, eyeing the front door.

Tate comes in, holding my glass. Sigrid passes the popcorn. "Hickory-barbecue," she says. "Hope you like it."

"Thanks," I say weakly and scoop up a big handful. It's got a real bite, so I tuck in. The Cherry Coke's too sweet for my taste, but I'm thirsty, and the popcorn makes me thirstier. I'm drawn right into the movie. Carrie's an only child and an outcast, except she's got a crazy mother instead of a drunk one. The girls in school are mean to her, especially after they're handed a detention that they blame on her.

When Sigrid fills my glass again, I scarcely notice, chugging the Coke and stuffing my face with popcorn. To my amazement, I'm having fun. I've never in my life watched a video with two other girls.

Turns out Carrie has some weird powers that take her by surprise. I sure like the way she defies her mother and sews a dress for the prom she's been forbidden to go to.

She looks so pretty, and the decorations at the prom are great—glittery stars and globes of colored light. Even though I know something awful's going to happen, I'm hoping her date will rescue her.

The two of them start to dance, the music slow and romantic. They turn around and around, the colored lights twirling, the stars glittering, faster and faster—and right on cue I begin to feel dizzy, the couch swaying as if it's a hammock, the overhead light dipping up and down. I close my eyes. The couch does an almighty swoop. Someone laughs.

I just about jump out of my skin, then I realize it's Tate. Feeling real foolish, I take another slurp of Coke, sneaking a glance at her. She's watching the screen, didn't even notice.

Suddenly there's three Tates, each one wavering like the lights. Three Tates, three screens, and the floor under my feet isn't behaving the way a floor's supposed to. A longing to be home in my own bedroom seizes hold of me.

I lever myself up from the couch. My knees won't carry me, which is when I notice Tate grin at Sigrid, dig her hand under the cushion, and take out a digital camera. As I stagger to my feet, braced against the arm, she points it at me and the flash goes off. Pinpricks of color explode in my brain.

"What—what's up?"

"Little souvenir of a girls' night out," Tate says.

"I don't feel so good." Except *sho* is what I say. "I gotta phone me da."

Pushing off from the arm of the couch, I stand up. The room whirls around me, then I'm falling. Next thing you know, I'm draped over the cushions, which smell of stale cigarette smoke, and Tate's got the camera stuck in my face as if she's interviewing me.

"Tell us what you think of the movie."

"Or how much you liked the Cherry Coke," Sigrid adds with a laugh that slashes right through me.

I'm drunk.

I won't puke. I won't.

My arms and legs seem to belong to someone else, but my mind's on fast-forward. Tate will get Sigrid to post the photos on Facebook and tell the kids at school to check them out. *Look at Prinny Murphy, takes after her ma...*

Facebook's the kiss of death. And what if Da finds out? Or Aunt Ida? Can terror sober you up?

I moan, which isn't hard to do. Keeping my head down, I shove against the cushion and half-fall, half-roll to the floor. Laminate. Cold on my cheek. Dust bunnies galore. Alls I want to do is stay here.

When I raise my head, moaning again, I see Tate's moved back a bit to get the whole picture in: couch, floor, and a tanked-out-of-her-mind Prinny Murphy.

"What was in the Coke?" I mumble, slurring the *s* in *was*.

Tate laughs this time. "Vodka. No taste to it, plus there was all that cherry flavor," she says. "Smile for the camera, Prinny."

"You gotta help me up…don't wanna barf all over the floor."

I make a retching noise and then I'm ice-cold, terrified I really am going to upchuck. Sweat springs out on my forehead. I swallow hard. That bitter taste, nastiest taste I know, slides back down my throat. But Tate's scowling at me, and Sigrid—only one of her, not three—looks real agitated.

"I don't want her throwing up on the floor," she says. "I ain't cleaning it up. I told you to slack off on the vodka."

"Bathroom's thataway," Tate says, the flash going off in my face again.

As Sigrid grabs me by the shoulder and hauls me upright, I lean on her, no faking involved. She holds herself rigid, warding me off like I'll contaminate her. "Tate, quit waving that camera around," she snaps. "I don't plan to be in any of them photos."

"Let's take a picture of her with her head in the can," Tate says.

We stumble to the bathroom, waves of sickness washing over me. Sigrid bangs up the lid and the seat. The toilet could do with a good dose of Javex. I let go of Sigrid, crash into Tate, grip her wrist to steady myself, then rip my nails across her skin and watch the camera fall into the toilet bowl.

Kerplop.

My hand darts out and shoves the handle down. The toilet begins to flush. Sigrid makes a sound like someone's choking her. Tate screeches, "Fish it out!"

"Gross. It's your camera—you fish it out!"

I lunge for the bathroom door, bash my shoulder on the frame, and rebound into the living room. My knee cracks into the corner of the coffee table. Pain spurs me across the room, the front door looming like the gateway to Heaven.

The back door scrapes open. A man bellows, "You here, Sigrid?"

Lorne. Sigrid's brother. Home early. I grab my jacket from the hook and I'm out the door and down the path quicker than you can say *vodka*. It's not dark yet, although lights are shining in some of the houses. Makes me feel safe; Sigrid and Tate can't drag me back indoors with everyone watching.

Not that I want anyone watching. No point in that camera ending up in the john if all the neighbors spy me drunk as a kite.

Tate's camera in the john. Me responsible. Omigosh.

Walking a straight line appears to be a skill I've lost. I stare at the edge of the road, blanking out everything except the painted white line, the one that shines in the dark. Why can't I make my feet do what I'm telling them to do?

Because they're not listening. Is this how Ma feels when she spends the day at the tavern? Sick to her stomach, her body like it belongs to an ugly stranger, her mind flitting from here to there as if every surface is too scary to land on? I can't imagine doing this to yourself for fun. For kicks.

I waver off the edge of the road onto the shoulder, lose my balance, and tumble into the ditch like a sack of bones. As rocks dig into my face, I start to cry, the tears hot against the cold, wet dirt. Snow's melting into my sneakers, soaking my ankles.

A car goes past; the driver doesn't even see me. Dimly I realize this is a good thing.

Waiting until everything's quiet again, the only sound the slosh of waves on the shore, I scramble up the far side of the ditch and dive into the trees. The snow's deeper here, and pretty soon my feet are dead cold. But when I clutch trunks and branches for support, the scent of spruce is familiar, comforting.

The trees thin out beyond Hud's place, which is the last house before the road winds its way to Ratchet. Ravens are complaining on the barrens; the sun's dipping toward the Blue Hills. Very carefully, I slide down the ditch and back onto the highway. Although my stomach's settled a bit, my head's still floating like a dory on a swell. Each step I take, my sneakers squelch.

At least I'm not singing. Or giggling, like Ma does when she's half cut.

Nothing much to giggle about. If they were giving out prizes for stupidity, guess who'd win the gold cup.

Some lucky I managed to dump that camera. Back in April, Sigrid posted pictures of Avery Quinn picking his nose, and Kim Corkum making out with Leo Dunstable behind the arena.

Prinny Murphy barfing popcorn and vodka? No thanks.

Six

be·'tray·als

I hear a car coming and do my level best to walk straight. *Level best*, ha.

The car stops and the window rolls down. "Want a drive, Prinny?"

It's Mr. Baldwin, who owns Baldwin's Store in Ratchet. Ma used to take me there when I was little so she could stock up on booze; he'd slip me a couple of jawbreakers or some gummy bears, like he was saying, *this will make you feel better.* And sometimes it did.

So I climb in. He rattles the paper bag that's between the two front seats. "Toffees in there. Help yourself."

My stomach heaves. "Not right now," I mumble. He's got the radio on, country and western, which saves me from talking. It's only three miles to Ratchet.

The car's looping around the turns. The black rosary beads dangling from the front mirror sway in circles. I can't imagine confessing to Father Gogan that I got drunk on cherry-flavored vodka on a Friday afternoon.

Mr. Baldwin stops at the bottom of his driveway. "You take care now, Prinny," he says and smiles at me. His teeth are brown because he chews tobacco; he spits into a soup can he keeps under the counter in the store.

"Thanks, Mr. Baldwin," I whisper, pushing back more tears.

I get out of the car. A four-minute walk to my place, then I'm home safe. I should've asked Mr. Baldwin to drive me all the way. I bet he would have. But where he's so nice, I don't like to take advantage.

I brush some of the dirt off my jacket and straighten my shoulders. *Go, girl.*

The road's still acting more like a live snake than a road. I set off down the hill, praying no one's peering out their window. Hector's mum, for instance. Her tongue never stops from wagging.

Two kids climb over the rocks onto the pavement.

Travis and Laice. Frantic, I look around for a place to hide.

"Prinny!" Travis yells. "Is that you?"

No. It's Santa Claus. Or the Blessed Virgin. Who does he think it is?

He's running up the hill, Laice close on his heels. I want to dive into the sea and swim all the way to Labrador. I want to melt into a puddle on the ground. Now he's standing five feet away, not even puffing because he's in such good shape from hockey. He says, suspicious as Da on one of his bad days, "What happened to your jacket?"

"I fell down."

"Did someone push you? Was it Sigrid?" As I shake my head, he eyeballs me like he's the lawyer for the prosecution. "You've been crying."

"So what if I have?" To my horror, *so* comes out *sho* again.

Laice steps closer. "She's slurring her words—she's drunk!"

She. Like I don't even exist.

"Prinny, have you been drinking?" Travis says. "Are you nuts?"

"I didn't—"

"Even if Tate offered it to you, you should have had more sense than to take it."

I could describe the Cherry Coke and the spicy popcorn, and how I managed to dump the camera in the toilet. Maybe if it was just Travis, I would have. But with Laice standing there, Little Miss Perfect, my lips clamp together like two halves of a clamshell.

"What are you planning to tell your dad?" Travis says. "He'll be afraid you're turning out like your mother."

"I'm not!"

"Looks to me like you are."

My voice trembles. "That's the meanest thing you could've said to me."

Now I'm not going to explain what happened. Ever.

Quick as it bared its teeth, my anger collapses. I gotta get out of here. If I blubber in front of Laice, I'll never forgive myself. But when I try to walk around them, I trip over the edge of the road, and there goes whatever dignity I had left.

I wobble down the hill. As I turn into our driveway, Travis and Laice are standing like stumps on the side of the road. Da's truck is parked by the house; the lights are on in the shed. I stand outside it, call, "I'm home, Da," and make a dash for the front door.

I'm nearly there when Da pokes his head out of the shed. "There's stew left," he hollers.

"It's okay. I ate."

I stumble indoors. I'm crying again.

The tears get drowned in the shower, where I scrub my skin until it's red and lather shampoo into my scalp. Then I brush my teeth and gargle twice with mouthwash. For my birthday I was given some smelly body lotion, so I slather that on. Last, I put on clean pajamas.

When Da comes in the house, me and my two cats are in bed. Tansy is stretched out beside me, while Rogue is on the pillow; his purr sounds like Da's outboard on full throttle.

Footsteps thud down the hall and stop outside my door, which is shut tight. "You awake, Prinny?"

"I have a headache, Da. I took some aspirin." I'm lying, of course; I figure the headache's holding off until tomorrow. Just the same, it seems stupid, us talking through a closed door. "You can come in," I say.

Even though I'm feeding him good, Da's lost weight since he kicked Ma out. But he still fills the doorframe. Winter and summer, he wears a T-shirt, overalls, and gray wool socks knit by Mrs. Baldwin at the store.

"It's nice you got invited out," he says. "Kids from school?"

I nod. My head spins. "We watched a video."

Rogue stands up, turns in a circle, and plops down again. "Them cats keep you good company."

I pick Tansy up, planting a kiss between her ears where the fur's soft. She wriggles, batting at me with her paw. Careful not to slur the *s*, I say, "I'm some glad you let me have them."

I've never told him that before. He says, "Travis kept on at me until I couldn't say no."

I don't want to talk about Travis. "Anyways, thanks, Da. I love Tansy and Rogue."

He shuffles his feet. "Time for wrestling on TV," he says, and backs out the door, shutting it smartly behind him.

Ma's drinking never made him none too happy. Quite a while ago he quit smoking, as though to show her quitting could be done; and he often used to drop Alcoholics Anonymous into the conversation. But the last couple years, he did nothing. Let her ride all over him and kept coming back for more. When she smashed the TV and he threw her out, it was a toss-up who was the most shocked: Da, Ma, or me.

His only daughter into the vodka? Bad scene.

In the morning, the headache's caught up with me. Jackhammer between my ears. Vise tight around my forehead. I take four Tylenol.

The chores loom like a month's worth of dirty dishes. I hang a load of wash on the line, clean the bathroom, and take pork chops out of the freezer for dinner. I'm going out on the barrens. Not enough snow left for snowshoes, so I wear my rubber boots.

As I start out, the Blue Hills beckon to me, the way they always do. The only books I ever take out of the school library are field guides to shrubs, trees, birds, and mammals. By sticking to the pictures I've been able to name most everything I see out here, although I often wish I could read the descriptions.

My problems with reading started back in grade one when Ma first hitched herself to Captain Morgan Rum. Tantrums. **Blackouts.** Puke. Flies buzzing around the food on the counter, dirty underwear piled on the washer. School should have been a haven, but it was like I was split in two—half of me home, terrified of what was going to happen next, the other half in the classroom with the red and blue desks, terrified of vowels and consonants.

Sometimes I was expected to stay home and look after Ma, especially when Da was off fishing. Sometimes, if she was screaming and yelling at Da, I'd stay in bed, huddled under the covers, and they'd never even notice I hadn't gone to school. *Absenteeism* was a word I learned young. I also learned to skulk in the back row of the class, pretending to be invisible.

The dead spruce trees in the hollows look like piles of antlers. An onshore wind scuds clouds across the sky. The air smells of peat and salt, and of the bayberry leaf I've crushed between my fingers.

One of my problems is not knowing where I belong. The barrens when I'm on my own, that's easy. It's the rest I can't handle. Recess. The rink. The school bus. Anyplace there's kids who can't see past my ma to me, Prinny Murphy.

Last night Travis joined those kids.

The hockey finals are tonight, St. Fabien Furies versus the Blandings Polar Bears. What if Sigrid and Tate are there? Laice is bound to be. The other person who'll be there, of course, is Travis.

* * *

Once I'm home, I ask Da if he'll drive me to five o'clock Mass at Our Lady of the Reefs, which is in Fiddlers Cove. He's fine with that—means he can sleep in on Sunday. He quit church after Father Gogan came to the house dropping hints that Ma would be happier if she and Da had a couple more kids to keep her busy.

Funny thing, that. If they'd had more kids, I might have a sister. Someone who'd take away the emptiness. Not often I find myself on Father Gogan's side of the fence.

Father Gogan has a face as long as misery—he's not the reason I go to church. Near the altar, there's a wooden statue of the Virgin Mary carved by a guy from Blandings. He painted her robe sea blue and her veil foam white. Her neck isn't meekly bent, the way it usually is; she's looking straight at you, her eyes the same sea blue, her gaze steady. *You do your part*, she says, *and I'll do mine*.

So here I am, sitting near the front so I can see her, scarcely paying attention to the service because I'm praying so hard. *Please don't let anyone spread the word that I was drunk. Not at the rink. Not at school. Not on the bus. Please don't let anyone...* I breathe in the familiar smells of varnished wood and old hymn books; the pews creak, the red vigil lamps flicker and glow.

Someone kicks me in the ankle. I blink, stand up, and shuffle up the aisle to receive the Host. Then I'm back in the pew with my mind gone blank, and next thing you know I'm mumbling good evening to Father Gogan and hurrying down the church steps.

I arrive late at the rink on purpose. The first person I see is Tate, both hands loaded with fries from the canteen. She walks right up to me, and for a crazy moment I think she's going to smush the fries in my face. She says, "You ruined my camera—even though Sigrid fished it out of the toilet, it's done for."

She's half my size, yet I'm shivering like a beaten dog. She'll tell the whole world I was drunk. Nothing I can do to stop her.

I try to remember the Virgin's steady eyes. "I wouldn't have gone near your camera if you hadn't been taking pictures of me. But Da's been hurt bad by my ma—photos of me drunk would finish him off."

"You're gonna pay for a new camera. Cash. Up front."

"I can't do that! Cameras are expensive."

"Sorry now you flushed the toilet?" Her eyes are cold as sea-glass. "I wants a bigger zoom than on my old one. I'll price a couple models and get back to you."

"When?" I croak.

"When I'm ready."

"Your fries are getting cold," I mutter, rub the wing bone in my pocket, and watch her march off toward the bleachers.

I need fries after that. Hot, greasy, drowning in gravy.

At the canteen, Laice and Joan are the last ones in the line-up. I hesitate just too long. Laice turns around and sees me, and with a sick thud in my chest, I realize what she's wearing. A black hockey jacket, TRAVIS embroidered in gold on the shoulder, St. Fabien Furies written across the pocket. It's his new jacket, the one his dad gave him for Christmas. He's right proud of that jacket, told me so himself.

Laice smirks at me. "Hi, Prinny," she says. "Are you feeling better?"

"I'm fine."

"How come you're not wearing Travis's old jacket?"

"I'm mad at him."

She wasn't expecting me to say that. She steps closer, lowering her voice. "Travis and I are going steady."

So he gave her the jacket because he's crazy about her. Head over heels in love. But isn't your head always over your heels? Heels over head in love would make more sense.

At the counter, Joan says, "Gravy on your fries,

Laice?"

Laice shakes her head, the light gleaming in her curls. "Aren't you going to congratulate me and Travis, Prinny?"

Stubbornness rises in me, Da's stubbornness, solid as a reef. "You're congratulating yourself plenty. You don't need me."

"Where's your money?" Joan says impatiently, thrusting a tray of fries at Laice.

Laice slaps some coins into Joan's palm, giving me one last smile. "After Travis's team wins their game tonight, we're going to a party. But I'll only be drinking pop."

Then she and Joan walk away. As I step up to the counter to order fries with gravy, I feel shaky inside, the way I used to feel when Ma went on a binge. It was never anything romantic between me and Travis, don't get me wrong. But he was my best friend—well, let's be honest, my only friend—and I guess without really knowing it I'd assumed that once we were older, fourteen or fifteen, we'd be the ones going steady.

Hector's sitting by himself at one end of the bleachers. "Okay if I sit here?" I say.

"Sure."

He has fries as well, and a Coke, dark brown and fizzy. I look the other way. Three rows down, Laice is sitting beside Joan, talking up a storm. About me?

Give Laice credit: at the canteen Joan didn't seem to know anything about last night. But if I'd wanted the secret kept, I should've been nicer to Laice.

I've tried *nice* at school. Turning the other cheek only gets you slapped twice.

SEVEN

ex·'tor·tion

The final game of a tournament on home ice when your team's winning is real neat. I manage to get into the spirit of the game, hollering and whooping with the rest. Hector even raises a yell or two, and groans out loud when the ref makes a bad call. The St. Fabien Furies win 6-5, Travis scoring three of those goals with two assists, and the crowd goes crazy. Been four years since our team won any kind of banner; it'll look some pretty hanging from the rafters.

Only sour face I see is Hud's. He plays defense, hardly ever scores a goal, which is another of the reasons he hates Travis. Plus, Travis is too much of a scrapper to back down; I figure Hud has to keep at him in hopes that sooner or later Travis will cry uncle.

Some hope.

Hector and I edge our way outside. Da's waiting in the truck; Hector drives off with his parents. All the way home, I try not to think about Travis and Laice going to a party.

Going steady.

At least nobody at the rink knew about last night. Same holds true at school on Monday. Not a breath about me being drunk as my ma. Instead, the buzz is that Mrs. Dooks's brother from Blandings is real sick with lung cancer. So I do my best in remedial reading, working my way through *land'slide*, *res'cue* (by the perfect dog Ben), and *bur'ied treas'ure*. Most of the time Mrs. Dooks is staring out the window. When I finish, she says, "Good, Prinny."

Good? At reading? *Me?* "I'm sorry about your brother, Mrs. Dooks."

"Thank you," she says, just like I'm a grown-up.

If I was grown-up, I'd do away with remedial reading.

At recess Tuesday, I'm standing by the fence gazing across the street when, right behind me, a raspy voice says, "You and me need to have a talk."

My hair's long, so it can't very well rise on the back of my neck. But my nape gives this little shiver. Slowly I turn around.

Tate's holding out a computer printout with a picture of a camera on it. "$149.95 plus tax," she says. "I'm feeling generous—I'll pay the tax."

The shiver turns into a chill that races all the way to my toes. "A hundred and fifty *dollars*?"

"We'll start with fifty."

"I don't have that kind of money! You think I'd be wearing these boots—or this jacket—if fifty-dollar bills floated around my place?"

"Even without the photos, Sigrid could make a real good story out of Friday night."

"I'll pay for a cheaper camera, one like you had."

"That's not the kind I want."

Then Tate fishes an envelope from her pocket. *Thomas Murphy*, it says, which is Da, and the address is ours. When I reach for it, she snatches it back. "Not so fast."

She pulls two photos out of the envelope and waves them in front of me. Ma, in what looks like a tavern or a club, laughing, lipstick a red slash. The same man draped over her in each picture, and he's not Da. He has a stupid little beard. Tate says, "I plan on mailing these to your father."

"Where'd you get those? You said your camera was fried."

"Sigrid's brother took them at one of the clubs. Your father oughta know what's going on, wouldn't you say?"

"You mustn't send them to him!"

"Watch me." She tucks the photos back in the envelope and sticks it in her pocket. "Let's cut to the chase, Prinny. Fifty bucks tomorrow and the rest later. If you pay up tomorrow, I won't mail these to anyone—I'll tear them up."

"Tomorrow," I repeat numbly.

"You're into protecting your dad. You told me that at the rink—you should learn to keep your mouth shut." Tate smiles, a smile so full of menace that I press back into the fence. "Tough luck your ma prefers the bottle to him. Get the money—steal it if you have to. Or I'll mail worse than these."

So there's more. "I can't do it by tomorrow—you gotta give me more time. Friday, at least."

"I make the rules here."

I scrabble for even a smidgen of Da's stubbornness. "Fifty bucks on Friday's better than nothing on Wednesday."

"Don't get too big for them boots of yours. Are you forgetting Facebook? If Sigrid posts these, everyone'll know about your ma—not just your dad."

I wilt. She says, "I must be in a good mood—Friday it is. Fifty bucks, no excuses, no delays—you wouldn't want me to set Mel on you."

All through Social Studies and Language Arts I'm in a funk. On the bus I don't even notice Travis and Laice, and I have a hard time concentrating on my cooking lesson with Rayleen.

At home, Da's in the kitchen brewing his tea. We learned in geography how the Japanese have a tea ceremony. Let me tell you, Da's a close rival: the pot warmed just so, loose tea measured out into a little metal container, which sits in boiled water for exactly ten minutes, then a few swishes before the tea gets poured into his chipped blue mug—the one he used on *Wilma's Dream*, the trap skiff he sold after the moratorium. Like his new boat, *Wilma Marie*, it was named after Ma, who's that scared of the water she never sets foot in a boat.

"Hi, Da," I say.

"Want some tea?"

"No thanks." I like the teabag waved over the mug and that's it. All of a sudden, words come out of my mouth, words I didn't even know I was thinking. "Do you still miss Ma?"

Did I really say that?

"Sorry, Da, sorry, forget it. I'll start supper in half an hour. We're having fish cakes."

"I wish she'd come home," he says.

Shoulders rounded, he's gazing into his mug as though he's liable to start crying into it any minute. Even though I'm ninety percent sure I don't want Ma home again, I say, "Sitting around moping won't bring her back."

"Wilma never did pay me much heed."

"You could change that, if you wanted to!"

I'm mad at Da? What's with me? He tugs at his ear.

"I told her the only way she could come back was if she quit drinking. Last I heard, that wasn't the case."

"You hear anything else?"

He scowls at me. "What are you getting at?"

So he doesn't know about the guy with the beard. "Drink your tea," I say, lug my books to my room, and dump them on the bed.

Then I open my dresser drawer, rummage under my socks, take out a brown envelope, and count the bills and coins. From the money Da pays me every week, I've saved $148.77. It's for the cats' shots, and to have them neutered once they're old enough.

I could pay for the whole camera on Friday.

Travis called me naïve last week when I thought Tate was being friendly, and he was right. But a deal's a deal, that's what Da always says; once the camera's paid for, that'd be the end of it. Likely Da would advance me extra money for the vet if I was caught short.

Yeah, that's what I'll do. Pay off the whole thing.

EIGHT

'dam·age con·'trol

Next day I stay in at recess and at noon sit with Hector in the canteen. I'm still not talking to Travis; it's a sorrow to me he's not making any moves my way.

After school, I don't get on the bus to go home; instead, I set out for Aunt Sebina's. She lives six blocks from the school.

Ma has three sisters altogether. Aunt Bethana went out west when she turned sixteen and never came back, not even for a visit. Uncle Doyle's the only brother. He's the reason I always wanted a sister.

Partway to Aunt Sebina's, I go past the mall and guess what—there's Ma coming out of FoodMart, lugging four bags of groceries. She's walking a straight line for once.

I wave at her and hurry over. Her hair's clean; she smells of Avon's "Sweet Honesty." "Want me to take a couple of bags?" I say.

"Your da? He okay?" she says sharply.

"He's fine."

"Then what are you doing here?"

"I need to talk to you."

She passes over two of the bags. "You can walk and talk at the same time."

"One of the girls at school has photos of you in a tavern. Drinking—with this guy with a beard. She's going to mail them to Da and post them on Facebook if I don't come up with a wad of cash by Friday."

"That's blackmail!"

"I want you to write Da a note, which I'll take home with me. Explaining that the guy isn't anything to you."

"What if he is?"

I wince. "Then lie. You're good at that."

"I don't—" Ma stops and sighs. "We always end up squaring off, you and me."

"You got that right." The bags are heavy, the plastic cutting into my fingers.

"Let me get this straight," Ma says. "I write a note for your Da, you don't give the girl any money, and my photo ends up on the Internet."

"And sent to Da. Or did you forget that?"

"You figure he'd care?"

"Ask him. Not me."

Ma sighs again. "The booze...it makes me right foolish."

"So, give it up."

"Yeah...just like that."

I stop dead on the sidewalk, the wind blowing in my face. "Why do you need to drink, now you're not living with Da and me?"

"It's not that simple, Prinny."

"You make it complicated!"

Her voice sharpens. "There's stuff you don't know anything about."

"Oh sure—any excuse so you won't have to quit."

"You're always so angry with me!"

I don't say anything because if I open my mouth, heaven knows what'll spew out. She takes a deep breath, trying to calm down. "Are other kids at school mean to you because of me?"

"Sometimes."

"I been dry for three days. Scared myself over the weekend. Woke up in a backyard somewheres out of town and didn't have a clue how I got there. Shocked me sober, it did."

"The guy in the photo—was he there?"

She drags in another lungful of air, avoiding my eyes. "He's just a drinking buddy."

Somewheres—somewhere—deep down I'd been hoping Tate's pictures had been photo-shopped, the whole thing a fake. "There's a *thou shalt not* about adultery."

"I told you, alls we did is share a few drinks—

nothing happened!" she says, sharp-like. "And you might want to remember there's a *thou shalt* about honoring your mother—try it some time."

"How am I supposed to do that, Ma?" I say, and even I can hear the pain in my voice. "Maybe you have to honor yourself first. Maybe I can't do it for you."

She's staring at me like I just sprouted six heads. "I wouldn't know where to begin," she whispers. "I never got honored when I was little. But your da honored me—that's why I married him. Turned out to be not enough, but how was I to know?"

Ma's never backward in spilling her guts when she's drunk; but sober, that's something new. "Write me the note. Then I can catch the late bus home."

"I got no paper."

I stop, put down the groceries, and scrabble in my pocket, taking out a pen and a folded piece of paper. She says bitterly, "You thought of everything."

"Somebody has to."

She lifts a box of cereal from one of the bags, rests the paper on it, thinks a moment, then writes. When she's done, she passes me the paper. I squint at it. *Tom*, it says, *if you see photos of me, don't pay no attention. He's a drinking buddy, that's all. Wilma.*

No *Dear Tom*. No *Love, Wilma*. "Thanks," I say, jamming it in my pocket any which way. "The last bus'll be leaving—can you manage the groceries?"

"Prinny…"

I'm so scared she'll try to kiss me that I almost throw the groceries at her. Our hands touch. I turn tail and run.

The bus takes me home via the back of beyond. I'm in a funk again, the emptiness as bad as it's ever been.

If I had a sister, she wouldn't have been naïve enough to drink Cherry Coke and vodka.

By Friday morning the funk's worse. Tate doesn't make a move on the bus. But at recess, slick as can be, the Shrikes trap me against the fence. Tate says, "Where's the money?"

I pass her an envelope. She pulls out three tattered ten-dollar bills and two fives, and rattles the loonies and toonies. Fifty dollars all told. "So you're not as stupid as you look," she says.

She doesn't know how I sat on my bed this morning counting all my bills and coins, fifteen weeks of cooking and cleaning at ten dollars a week.

Then I stared at the money for a long time.

Maybe I am stupid. If I'd paid the whole amount, she'd be off my back. But all that hard work just so Tate Cody can have a bigger zoom?

The words come from nowhere. "I had to lift ten dollars from Da's wallet. If he figures out where it went, I'm in big trouble."

The perfect family with their perfect dog Ben are one big lie. If books can do it, so can I. I even feel a tiny jolt of excitement because I'm getting away with it.

Mel seizes my wrist with both hands, one hand twisting one way, one the other. Pain hot as fire.

"Next week," Tate says. "Same time, same place, second installment. Fifty bucks."

Before they walk away, she tosses the two photos of Ma on the ground. My breath escapes in a long sigh. I cradle my wrist; the skin's bright red. I've bought time, and that's all I've done.

When push came to shove, I couldn't give Ma's note to Da—I couldn't face the thought of him seeing those photos.

Nine

e·'piph·a·ny

Mrs. Dooks's brother has taken a turn for the worse, so last period we have a substitute for English, a young guy in jeans and a T-shirt. His name's Mr. Roberts. Looks like he lifts weights, which makes the boys pay attention, and he's seriously cute, which makes the girls sit up straight. When Brad Wadley tries to push his buttons, Mr. Roberts puts Brad in his place right smart.

Then he says, "I know it's Friday afternoon and you all want to be out of here...I'm going to read to you from two books, both young-adult novels, one written in prose, one in free verse—I'll put the pages on the screen as we go. Then we'll talk about which one you prefer."

The first book is about a boy whose mother disappears after they're evicted from their apartment; the second one's about a girl living in a city slum who looks after two little kids so their seventeen-year-old mother can go to work.

Both books are so different from the perfect dog Ben

that I sit bolt upright. These stories are real, the stakes so high my brain's wide-eyed. As Mr. Roberts keeps reading, everything else in the room disappears. Even the voice isn't his anymore. He becomes Heck, sleeping in a car, broke and hungry. He becomes LaVaughn, who babysits in a building alive with cockroaches, where the stairways reek of pee; she has a mother who's a Big Mom, a force to be reckoned with.

It's not just the girls who keep quiet; the boys do, too. I never knew books could be like that, take you inside them so you vanish. I gotta have that book, that *Make Lemonade*, so I'll know what happens to LaVaughn.

I'm glued to the screen, which shows the page he's reading. Short lines, each word clearly itself and nothing else, the *l*'s and *d*'s standing tall, the *s*'s curving, the *o*'s perfectly round. It all rushes in and fills the emptiness, that page inside me with no words on it.

I can hardly bear it when he stops reading. He's asking questions now, and everyone but me is in a hurry to answer. Then the bell rings. Usually on Fridays the doorway's mobbed. But today kids linger, the boys arguing about what Heck should have done, the girls surrounding Mr. Roberts.

How am I going to get near him? The bus leaves in ten minutes.

He catches sight of me, standing dumb as a lobster

at the back, and beckons me forward. As the bell rings again for the first buses, some of the kids wander out. I walk up to him. There's a thin, high singing in my head. "The lemonade book, is it in the library?"

"No," he says, "not at school or in town—I checked."

Disappointment rises harsh in my throat. He says, smiling at me, "You liked it?"

"Does it work out okay for her? LaVaughn?"

He says, "Would you like to have my copy? I have another one at home."

"For *keeps*?" He nods. "But I don't read so good— I'm in remedial reading every Monday. I don't even like books!"

"All the more reason you should have this one." When he picks it up from the desk and passes it to me, my fingers close around it as if I already knew the way it would feel. "Why don't you find someone to read to you?" he says. "One or two chapters at a time. It can be very helpful if you're having difficulties."

"Like you read to us? I sure liked that."

I clasp the book to my chest, blinking back tears, me who never cries in school. The last bell rings. "I better run or the bus will leave without me. I—thank you, Mr. Roberts. Thanks a million."

Who can I ask to read to me? Not Da. Only thing he reads is newspapers. Travis would've been the obvious choice, before Laice came along and before he insulted me so deep. If Laice was nicer I could ask her—she's a real good reader. Hector? He liked the Heck book better than the lemonade one, he actually spoke up in class and said so. As for Aunt Ida, she cleans house and sews wrap-around skirts for Ethiopian orphans; she thinks reading's a waste of time.

I can read to myself. I'll manage.

I race through supper and break a speed record washing the dishes. Da says, "How about you make a list and we do groceries, Prinny?"

"Now?"

"I'm at the wharf all day tomorrow, mending my pots."

Scowling, I go for my jacket.

In St. Fabien, Da goes to Home Hardware to buy lathes while I swing up and down the aisles in the grocery store, checking off the list at a great rate. Then who do I see but Father Gogan, clutching a bottle of salad dressing by the throat.

"Prinny," he says, "are you here by yourself?" I shake my head.

His smile needs 3-In-One Oil. His jacket's open; my eyes fall to his crucifix. Jesus dying in agony, muscles like knots. My scalp crawls. I like the smoothed-over Jesuses better.

Father Mortimer was our last priest. He was young. We used to have guitars in church, and he could make the rules slide down easy as OJ. With Father Gogan, those same rules tend to stick in my craw.

"Where's your father?" he says.

"In Heaven?" I reply, all wide eyes and innocence.

"Your earthly father," he snaps. Then, as Da's boots clump around the corner, he smiles again. "Thomas…seems I have to come to FoodMart to see you. For certain I never see you at Mass."

"No, Father."

"And Wilma?" He looks up and down the aisle. "Is she with you?"

Da presses his big hand on my shoulder. "No, Father."

"Well, at least I see Prinny once a week." He clasps the crucifix. "I sincerely hope you will urge Wilma to move back home—a woman's place is with her husband."

"Yes, Father."

Looking as mournful as Clarry Murphy's spaniel, Father Gogan raises his hand in blessing. Then he's gone. Da lets go of my shoulder and sighs. "Are we nearly done, Prinny?"

"We need mayo and bread, that's all."

"Let's get outta here."

At least we didn't bump into Ma in St. Fabien.

Maybe she's at Aunt Sebina's drinking ginger ale. Or maybe she's in one of the clubs, hoping that guy with the beard will open a tab for her.

As long as she stays out of my face, I don't care where she is.

It's nine-thirty by the time I'm settled in my room, Tansy in a neat ball on the pillow, Rogue sprawled on the spread with his chin resting on my ankle, his tail twitching. Tansy's ginger-colored. Rogue's gray with a black nose and white paws, and not that swift; perhaps he didn't get enough to eat when he was inside his mother's belly, her being a stray and all. So far I haven't let either of them out of the house. I want to be real sure they know this is home before they go outside.

Mr. Roberts put a bookmark at the beginning of the section he read. Although it's in the middle of the book, I decide that's where I should read, too; those eight pages were so strong, so real, it's almost as if I'd memorized them. Still, the first time through, there are lots of hitches, enough that I have to open my dictionary. The next two times I follow the words a bit easier, sounding them under my breath; on the fourth go-round they're suddenly not just words, all disconnected, they're the story and the story catches me up and carries me away, all eight pages of it. Just like in school.

Makes me breathless. Makes me so excited I have to slide out of bed and go into the kitchen to fix myself a peanut butter and jam sandwich. Da joins me, sniffing the air like a bear at the dump.

"Pass the bread," he says, and gobs peanut butter on it. "You look some pleased with yourself."

Before you know it, I'm telling him about Mr. Roberts and how much I love this book that I can read way better than anything else I ever tried because it has short lines and I really like LaVaughn. He munches on the sandwich, his squinched-up eyes showing he's listening. I finish by mentioning Mr. Roberts's suggestion that I find someone to read to me.

"Never was much of a hand at reading, myself," Da says. "You should ask Travis to read to you. His da is a doctor, so he's gotta be smart. And he's your friend."

Da's right. Travis *is* my friend. Okay, so he blew it the other night. Blew it big-time. Maybe I have to get past that. Past that, and past Laice, too.

"I will ask Travis to help me, Da. Good idea."

He looks pleased. It occurs to me that silence is mostly what he's gotten from me since Ma moved out, and yelling was mostly what Ma dealt out before she left. A warm feeling curls around my heart, warm as Rogue and Tansy.

For a moment our eyes hold, mine and Da's. "Want some more bread?" I say foolishly.

"Nah. I'll watch the news and go to bed. Early start in the morning. You be okay on your own tomorrow?"

"I'll go over to Travis's, then I'll clean the kitchen and the bedrooms."

As though the words are a snare and he's the rabbit trying to decide whether to go ahead or back up, Da says, "You're a good daughter, Prinny."

A blush rises from my chin to my hairline. "Thanks," I mumble, watching him head for the TV.

After Ma smashed his flat screen, which was discounted because he worked Christmas shifts at Home Hardware, he bought a cheap TV from Walmart. Hurts me every time I see him glued to that little screen.

One of these days I'm going to get up my courage and give him a hug.

Not sure whether I'm avoiding Travis or hoping he'll be there, I go to Abe's barn early the next morning. Abe waves at me through the kitchen window as I walk past; I edge the barn door open, slip inside, then freeze. Ghost is perched on a corner post of the cow's stall. He's watching the cow; the cow is watching him.

Ghost's fur is whiter than Da's T-shirts. You can't see his ribs, which used to look like the bars of a cage.

Hay dust tickles my nose. Even though I clamp my mouth shut and swallow my breath, I sneeze anyway. Ghost leaps onto the pile of straw bales, streaks to the top one, and vanishes.

"We're both scaredy-cats, Ghost," I say. As the cow rubs her face on the post, her brass bell jangles.

No sign of Travis.

At eleven o'clock I'm knocking on Travis's door. Even though one of us has to make the first move and I've decided it's going to be me, I still feel lousy when I remember how he compared me to Ma. If he agrees to read to me, I'll be polite, I'll say thank you. But I won't fall all over him like Rogue does the moment you hand him a treat.

Travis's father opens the door. He's tall with messy hair and the sort of smile you'd like every doctor to have.

"Hi, Dr. Keating. Is Travis in?"

"He went over to Laice's half an hour ago. They were going to the mall with her grandparents, so I expect he'll be gone most of the day."

I don't know which is worse, the let-down or envy, hot and dark as Da's tea. "Can I help?" Dr. Keating says.

I'm already backing up. "I don't read so good, and I was planning to ask Travis to read me four or five pages of this book so I could practice on my own after. I'll—"

"Would I do instead?"

"You? But you're so busy—"

"Not right now. Come on in."

Five minutes later Dr. Keating opens *Make Lemonade*, starting on page one so I'll know how it all began. He reads six pages, three chapters altogether, me following along; for the first time, I realize how much harder this book is than Mrs. Dooks's easy readers. My heart sinks.

Dr. Keating says, "Would you like me to read it again? Slower, maybe?" Then he reads the pages once more.

"This LaVaughn," I say, "she's trying to make sense of what happens to her...I liked her from the get-go."

"I'll speak to Travis. I'm sure he'll be able to read to you from now on."

If Dr. Keating leans on Travis, I'll never know if Travis is reading to me because he's still my friend, or because his father told him to. Beggars can't be choosers; that's what Aunt Ida says when she's whipping up those skirts, and she's likely right.

"Maybe Travis won't have the time," I say. Now that he's so busy with Laice.

"I'll see that he does."

"Thanks a lot, Dr. Keating," I say politely. "I'll go home now and work on these pages myself."

In spite of his help, I slog through them like Mrs.

Dooks is perched on my shoulder. But if LaVaughn can plant lemon seeds so a tree will grow, I can make twenty-six letters sprout words.

From listening to Dr. Keating, there's a picture in my head of what's happening on each page. The words take shape, then start hanging together like friends in the schoolyard. Lines flow from one to the next, easier because they're short. Then the story takes me inside it and I don't even realize I'm reading.

In church, I've heard a lot about miracles. This one's my very own, so it's all the more miraculous.

TEN

short lines

It doesn't feel too miraculous the next afternoon when a knock comes on the door. Da's in the shed, so I go. Travis doesn't even look up to make sure it's me—although I don't suppose Da would be wearing pink slippers with the toes out.

"Hello, Travis," I say, snooty as Laice, which is how I plan to act until he apologizes. This is the first time he's been at the house since she arrived.

He says, "Now that hockey's over, I can read to you right after school three days a week. Mondays, Wednesdays, and Thursdays."

"Your father tell you to?"

He gives the doorstep a couple of good kicks. "So what if he did?"

"Travis," I burst out, "can't we be friends again? Even though you were mean to me and you're going steady with Laice?"

"Going *steady*?" he repeats, a blank look on his face. "Who told you that?"

I'll never have a better opportunity to diss Laice.

"Someone at school," I say vaguely.

"She kept on and on at me until I loaned her my new jacket," he says, scowling at the step. "I told her I'd never ask you to give the red one back."

"Oh. Why not?"

"Because you're my friend and she can like it or lump it." He jams his hands in his pockets. "I'm sorry I was mean to you about your mother, Prinny. I was way out of line."

A weight lifts off my chest. "Thank you," I say, as if he just handed me a Christmas present, gift-wrapped.

"So, yeah, Dad told me I had to read to you—but I was okay with it."

Another miracle. I'm on a roll. "Want to go out on the barrens? We could go to the fox den and see if the vixen comes out."

"That'd be cool."

The den isn't easy to find. You have to pass the ponds and follow a stream until you reach a small waterfall that's just a trickle in summer, then edge around the bog to a straggle of spruce trees. The den's on a rise hidden by the trees. When I go there, I always check to make sure no one's following me. The den's my secret.

Today there's no sign of the foxes, although a few fresh bones are scattered in front of the den. Being out here with Travis is like the times we used to go to Gulley Cove to feed the cats.

If two people are going steady but only one of them knows it, it doesn't sound too steady to me.

As we turn for home, I find myself telling him about the Cherry Coke and how Tate's camera ended up in the toilet. "I didn't set out to get drunk. Not like Ma."

"I should have known you wouldn't take a drink on purpose." He grins at me. "So sad about the camera."

Now's the time to confess about Tate and the money. But another name for Travis is Mr. Fix-It; if I mention blackmail he'll be gung-ho to blab to the principal, or Corporal Deakins at the RCMP. Wouldn't that bring the Shrikes down on me like a ten-ton truck.

"If I'd listened to you," I say, "I wouldn't have gone near Sigrid's."

"I'm a pro when it comes to bullies."

"Hud bothering you lately?" I ask.

Hud's bullying is the fists-and-boots type; photos wouldn't turn his crank.

"He didn't dare come near me in hockey season." Travis says. "The team would've killed him. And I hang pretty tight with Cole, Buck, and Stevie—even Hud wouldn't take on the four of us."

"His da is one mean cuss. As for his ma, when God was handing out backbones, He skipped her altogether—look, there's a ptarmigan."

On the way back, we see three more ptarmigan and some ravens. Travis goes home for supper, and I add vegetables to the ham that's simmering in a big pot on the stove.

If I had a sister, I could have told her about Tate and the fifty bucks. Sometimes all you want is someone to listen. No fixing required.

After supper, I read the first six pages of my book, then I haul out my old phonics worksheets from grade three, and pay close attention to the vowel and consonant combinations and syllable patterns in LaVaughn's short lines. Me loving the story makes all the difference in the world.

Mr. Roberts will be proud of me tomorrow.

When we go to English class, the substitute's an old guy who spends the whole period on grammar, stuff like *he lies down after he lays the book down*. I keep a low profile, wanting him to be Mr. Roberts so bad I could lie down on the floor and scream. Then Travis, when he comes over after school, reads the next five pages of the lemonade book like it's for girls and he'd rather lay it down to read about guys sleeping in cars.

Also he leaves me one page into a new chapter. Unlike his father, who read three entire chapters.

Travis is all I got. *Don't throw out cod tongues*

because you prefer cheeks—another of Aunt Ida's sayings. At least now I know what happens in those five pages. That'll keep me going until Wednesday.

Tuesday, Travis goes to Laice's, and Rayleen shows me how to make potato pancakes and poor man's pudding. After we grate the potatoes, they get added to the batter. As I flip the pancakes so they'll brown evenly, Rayleen says, looking at me sideways, "I don't see much of Travis these days. Off with Mattie and Starald's granddaughter half the time."

"He comes to my place three times a week to help me with reading."

"That Laice, she's real cute. According to Mattie, her parents are off on a cruise. For two months? There's more to it than that."

"If there is, Laice wouldn't tell me."

Rayleen starts peeling carrots. "Any word on your ma?"

I keep a grip on my temper. "She's staying in St. Fabien with Aunt Sebina."

"Your da planning on divorcing her?"

The metal spatula slips from my fingers and clatters to the floor. "*Divorce?*"

"That's the usual follow-up when you don't live together."

Ma divorced from Da. Gone forever. "The church wouldn't allow it."

"There's always annulment."

I bend over, pick up the spatula, and wash it in the sink. "How d'you tell when the pudding's done?"

"When the topping's fluffy and the sauce is thick...why wouldn't your da divorce her? She's useless as four legs on a hen."

She opens the oven door. A blast of heat hits me. You go to hell if you divorce...don't you? Not that Da has much time for church, Father Gogan, heaven, or hell.

Rayleen made enough pancakes for me to take some, and she divvies up the pudding. I hurry home, where I fry moose chops with onions. We sit down to eat. Da tucks in. I don't even taste the potato pancakes or the pudding. Just as he pushes back from the table, my mouth springs open. "You going to divorce Ma?"

He clunks down hard in the chair. "Divorce *Wilma*?"

"That's her name."

"Don't get lippy. And who gave you that idea?" He's starting to look angry. Da doesn't get angry often, but when he does he clings to it like a barnacle to a rock.

If I say Rayleen, he might put a stop to the cooking lessons. "Ma's been gone since November."

"I'm not giving my earnings to no crew of uppity lawyers."

The poor man's pudding is a lump in my stomach.

"Because we're Catholic?"

"Let it lay, Prinny!"

Lie, I think. *Let it lie*.

Just last week I was planning on hugging Da. Right now he looks as though he could grate me up for pancakes. "Sorry," I mutter, and gather up the dirty plates, my fingers clumsy, my heart stuttering in my chest.

I wish I could be LaVaughn and write stuff down in short lines so it would all make sense.

ELEVEN

'trin·i·ty

I hurry to the washroom after the noon bell. Drifts of toilet paper all over the floor, and the last person didn't flush. On the back of the metal door someone's printed, very neatly, *SCHOOL SUCKS*.

A couple of weeks ago I'd have totally agreed. But if it wasn't for school, I wouldn't know LaVaughn.

After flushing, I open the cubicle door, my mind on her, and there they are, lined up in a row facing me: tall, medium, short, like the three bears. No one else in the washroom. I start sidling in the direction of the door.

"Don't even try," Sigrid says sweetly.

Tate rasps, "We're here to remind you. Fifty bucks by Friday."

Today's Wednesday. I've been that excited about reading, my brain hit the Delete button on Tate's deadline. Bad idea to lose yourself in someone else's story when your own should have your full attention.

"I can't lay my hands on another fifty bucks."

"Steal it," Tate says.

"Da's no slouch—I'll never get away with that twice!"

She shrugs. "So the photos go on Facebook."

Mel plants herself in front of me. Before I realize what she's up to, she circles my throat with her big hands. Not squeezing, exactly. Just pressing. Almost gentle, until you see how much she's enjoying herself.

"You better get the money," she says. "You wouldn't want anything to happen to them cats of yours."

I say hoarsely, "They live indoors."

"Indoors. Outdoors. All the same to us."

"You wouldn't hurt my cats—you wouldn't be that mean!"

Mel digs her fingers in, enough so I can't breathe. Alls I can see is her eyes, cruel little eyes in a face that's too big for them. "Wanna bet?" she says. Then she lets go, brings her fists together, and twists them, like she's wringing a chicken's neck.

Or a cat's.

Tansy and Rogue. There's days I swear I love them more than I love Ma. And they love me back, I know they do.

"I'll get the money," I whisper.

Mel reaches out and tugs my ponytail so hard that tears spring to my eyes. "You do that."

"Yeah," says Tate, taking control again now that her muscleman's done the work. "You do that."

The three of them file out. I'm shaking so bad I

can hardly get my hand in my pocket, let alone wrap my fingers around the wing bone.

The rest of the day passes in a blur. The substitute teacher is on a punctuation kick, like where you put a comma really matters. Travis gets off the bus at my place because it's reading day. He rushes through five more pages and bolts out the door.

After I fix supper and put it down in front of Da, we eat in silence. He's not looking me in the eye. Still mad at me, I guess.

"Da, the whole street knows our front door key's under the shed step, and I worry someone might let the cats out. Can we find another place to hide it?"

"Where?" he says, gulping his tea.

"Why don't I leave it next door? They wouldn't mind. And will you remember to keep the front door locked?"

"Guess so," he says and leaves the room.

The last while it's as though anger's growing inside me, taller and taller, like the notches Da used to make in the door when I was four and five and six. No call for him to treat me like I'm the hired help.

After the dishes are done, I ask our neighbors to keep the key, and warn them never to give it to Mel, Sigrid, Tate, or Hud.

That should cover it.

Friday morning and we're piling off the buses. Diesel fumes billowing, engines snarling, kids yakking at the tops of their voices. From behind, someone shoves me against the back wheel.

Mel. Sigrid blocks me as I try to run. Tate holds out her hand.

I pull out a little roll of bills. "This is all I could come up with."

She counts them. "Thirty measly bucks—are you joking?"

I'm taking a big risk, and that's no joke. But with the front door locked, the cats are safe indoors.

"Walmart has cameras on sale for sixty-nine ninety-five," I say. "Nice cameras. There's enough here to pay the tax."

Tate says, "Next week. The twenty dollars you still owe from this week plus fifty more equals seventy dollars. The math's not difficult. Or Mel goes into action. She don't like cats."

Mel seizes my left arm, jerks it behind my back, and twists. My shriek is lost in the racket.

"Don't mess with us, Prinny," Tate says.

A grade-eight girl jostles me, doesn't bother to apologize. My anger grows another notch. Anger? Feels more like rage.

Rage plus fear equals a big mess. The math for that's not difficult, either.

Finally the last bell rings. I jam books from my locker into my backpack, making sure I have all my homework, and hurry to catch the bus. Then I lurch to a stop a few feet away. Ma's standing beside it. She's looking right at me.

The Shrikes are getting on the bus. Tate says in a loud voice, "It's Prinny's ma and guess what, she's sober," and the three of them giggle. Although Ma's face goes a mottled pink, she stands her ground.

Cole and Buck edge around her like they might catch something if they get too close. Laice does the same. But Travis says, even louder than Tate, "Hi, Mrs. Murphy, nice to see you. Prinny'll be along any minute."

Shame burns into me. Laice stares from Ma to him and back again; with a toss of her head, she climbs up the steps. My heels dragging in the dirt, I walk toward the bus. Mel's nose is pressed to the window. She waves at me, then says something to Sigrid that sends them into another fit of giggles.

Ma gives me a smile that's ragged around the edges. Tate's right; she's sober. "I won't keep you," she says.

"What d'you want?"

She tugs me away from the bus as a couple of other kids climb aboard. "Has your da seen them photos?"

"No."

"How come?"

I shake her hand off. "Because I shelled out the money."

"You can't do that!"

"I already did."

"Did they give you the photos?"

"What's the use? With digital, you can make more copies than there's starfish under the wharf."

Ma shrinks into her jacket like she's cold. "You mustn't give them any more money."

"I'll do whatever it takes to keep Da out of it." Tansy and Rogue as well, although I don't tell her that. I glare at her instead.

"You know who you remind me of?" she whispers. "Ida."

Me? Like Aunt Ida?

"Don't turn hard, Prinny," Ma says. "Hard is a terrible way to meet the world." Then she turns and walks away.

I'm left standing there like a moose that's been shot and doesn't have the wit to fall down. From inside the bus, Mr. Murphy calls, "Prinny? Time we were leaving."

I sit in the very front seat, staring out the window. I'm as different from Aunt Ida as I could be. Ma said that to get me riled up; she's always known how to push my buttons. I'm not hard. I cried buckets after she left, but she wasn't there to see it. She was having herself a fine old time in St. Fabien.

When I get home, I bang the pots around, plunk Da's supper in front of him, and chew like I've got her between my teeth. Da gives me one look and concentrates on his meatloaf and mashed potatoes. After supper, he goes over to Dave Baldwin's to play poker.

I'm restless as Tansy when the moon's full. Once I've washed the dishes, I head for the closet in the back room, the one I never got around to cleaning since Ma left. Rubber boots with holes in them, fishnet that's seen better days, three odd mittens, I turf them all out on the floor along with cans of rusty nails and a heap of *Good Housekeeping* magazines from five years back. Good housekeeping, I'll show you good housekeeping.

In a wooden crate near the back of the closet, I find two pints of Captain Morgan Rum. I dust them off, wondering why Ma prefers a black-haired pirate to her own husband and daughter.

Right after she left, I poured five bottles of booze down the drain, ones she'd hidden away for a rainy day.

I put the two bottles in the crate and leave the crate near the front of the closet.

TWELVE

'roll·er 'coast·er

The weekend moves at a crawl. Reading my book, doing the usual chores, going to church. Meeting Travis in Abe's barn and keeping my trap shut about blackmail. Worrying about Tate.

The rest of the time I spend near the fox den. I've been coming here since I was seven years old, so the foxes are like family. Every now and then the pups mew in the den. Twice I see the male bringing food to them and his mate; he's shedding his winter coat, his tail a thick brush tipped with white. His eyes gleam gold in the light.

First thing you know it's Monday and back to the grind. As I haul on my jacket to go to school, a seam splits under the arm. I don't have time to fix it; I'll just have to keep my arm tight to my side.

That night I'm leafing through the Sears catalogue when someone knocks on the front door. Da's in the shower, so I go. As I pull the door open, Uncle Ralph's car is driving away, two red tail-lights in the dusk. Ma's standing on the step, holding her suitcase. She bites her lip when she sees it's me.

"Aren't you going to invite me in?" she says.

"You've come home?"

"What does it look like? Where's your Da?"

"In the shower. Home to *stay*?"

She shoves at my knee with her case. "Let me in, Prinny. It's cold."

"But Da kicked you out," I say stupidly.

She shoves harder on the suitcase, I give her a bit of a push, then she plants her palm against my chest, thrusting me backward. I thud into the porch wall. Horrified, we stare at each other. All the years of her drinking, we never laid a hand on each other, not once.

"I didn't—"

"You can't—"

She snaps, "I'm home, okay?" She hangs up her coat, kicks off her boots, and waltzes into the living room like she owns the place. I follow, as if there's an invisible string between her and me.

She's wearing her good black skirt with a pink sweater. She looks young and pretty, her makeup soft, her lips frosted pink. She starts chattering away about the drive over, the price of gas, and Uncle Ralph's arthritis. She's nervous, I realize with a little stab of—of what?

The bathroom door opens, squeaking on its hinges.

Da comes clomping down the hall. Ma shuts up in mid-sentence, staring at the doorway like it's Judgment Day and St. Peter is going to flap into the room on wings of fire.

When he sees her, Da stops like he's run smack into a truck. In the space of a few seconds, his face goes from shock to joy to caution. But it's the joy that sticks with me. Da loves Ma, I think shakily. No way he'll ever divorce her.

After a pause that goes on too long, he clears his throat. "What's up, Wilma?"

"I wants to come home. If you'll have me."

He stares at her, not even blinking, no expression on his face at all now. "No booze in the house. No drinking."

"I been dry for fifteen days," she says. "That may not sound like much to you...but it's a lot. The first few days were something desperate. I didn't touch a drop, though—and now Dr. Keating's put me on a pill that makes me sick if I drink."

"You went to Dr. Keating? For help?"

"Past time, wouldn't you say?"

Suddenly Da's smiling. I've never seen him look like this, with so much love shining from his face. Ma's cheeks flush pink; she looks even prettier. They've both forgotten about me. He doesn't say anything, just walks up to her, wraps his arms around her, and holds her tight, like he's the one who's come home.

Ma closes her eyes. I slip past them, go to my bedroom, and shut the door.

All too soon, Ma taps on my door, pushing it open before I have the chance to say, "Come in." Her cheeks are still flushed and her lipstick's wore off.

She says, "Da and me have to talk to you. I made a pot of tea, why don't you come into the kitchen?"

My kitchen. "I'll be there in a minute," I say, and watch her hesitate before she turns around and disappears down the hallway. Mean of spirit, that's what I am, which Father Mortimer used to say was the worst of sins because it's the root of so many others.

In the kitchen Ma's put out mugs, milk, and sugar, as well as the cookies I baked on the weekend. I pour lots of milk into my tea because she's made it too strong. She says, "Look at me, Prinny."

I force my gaze up to meet hers. She says, "I'm going to do my best not to drink anymore. It'll be hard, and I'll need your help. I told your da about the blackouts and about the photos—so you don't have to worry about them."

Those photos have been the least of my worries.

Ma goes on. "I'll need stuff to do around the house to keep myself busy. So I'll make supper and your school lunches, and do the wash—"

"But I need the money Da's been paying me!"

"I know," she says, patiently for her. "If you wants to keep on with the cleaning and help with the groceries, your da'll pay you the same amount you've been getting all along." She smiles again, trying to win me over. "I never did care for the dust mop."

"The same amount of money for less work?"

Da says, "You can crew for me on weekends—we'll count that in."

"I want to cook dinner one night a week to practice the new recipes I get from Rayleen."

Before Da can say anything, Ma says, "Great... gives me a night off."

So that's that. I've been demoted and it's smiles all round.

Tuesday I go for my weekly cooking lesson, which keeps me out of Ma's road. But the following day, Travis reads five pages that end with everyone in an uproar except the cockroaches and LaVaughn. Even with the short lines, and even though I long to know what happens next, I lack the courage to try the following chapter on my own. So after I work on the five pages, I'm at a loose end.

Ma's in the kitchen, the radio on, humming away as she makes dinner. I sneak into the porch, pull on my jacket and rubber boots, and I'm out the door.

Maybe the vixen will come out of the den.

I'm only partway up the hill behind our place when I hear an animal crying, as though it's in pain. Several years back, Uncle Doyle used to set traps on the barrens, until council got wind of it and made him quit. I hurry toward the sound, praying I won't find a dog caught in a rusty old leg-hold. Not likely the fox would come this close to the houses.

The nearer I get, the less it sounds like an animal. I top the next rise. Laice is lying facedown on the crowberries, a piece of paper clutched in one hand. She's wailing as though her heart's broken.

I leap down the slope, the juniper springy underfoot. "Laice, what's the matter?"

Her body goes still. Then she raises her face. It's blotched with tears, her eyes swollen, her nose running. "Go away!"

"What's wrong? Has something happened to Travis?"

"You *would* think of him."

"Hud didn't get him, did he?"

"It's not *about* Travis." She pushes herself up on her elbows. "If you tell him you saw me, I'll make sure he never reads to you again. Not one single word."

"Don't you talk to me like that!"

"Don't tell me what to do."

"Just because my da's a fisherman, not the mayor of St. Fabien, doesn't mean I got no feelings."

Her breath catches on a sob. She gulps it back, rolls over, and sits up. The paper flaps in her hand; it's a letter. She looks down at it like she's not sure what it is. Although she's biting her lip hard, another sob bursts free.

My anger blows away. For the first time with Laice, I feel truly generous of spirit. "Did someone die?" I ask. Why else do people write letters?

"You think I'm going to share my private life with you? You're nothing to me, Prinny Murphy—you're less than nothing."

I say in a low voice, "I hoped we could be friends."

"I'm not that desperate." She scrambles to her feet, still clutching the letter, and wipes her face on her sleeve, smearing tears and snot across her cheeks. "Leave me alone, I don't want anything to do with you. I hate this horrible place, do you hear me? I hate you, too!"

At an awkward run she takes off along a caribou trail toward her house. Her blue jacket disappears through the tamarack. Inside me, anger, generosity, and hurt have swirled together into a big fat zero. No use thinking I'll ever have a girlfriend. The local kids wrote me off years ago; and if I needed proof Laice was a lost cause, I just got it.

Heartsore, I head for the fox den, where I tuck myself down in the bushes. Although I do my best to blank Laice out of my mind, I can't blank out the hatred. I wouldn't have thought I was important enough for her to bother hating me.

Twenty minutes later, the fox trots down the hill, three limp-bodied voles in his teeth. He's feeding his mate and his pups, looking after business the best way he knows how. In the den, the pups' mother is doing the same.

Animals aren't screwed up.

Okay, so I don't have a girlfriend, and no prospects of finding one. Nothing new there. But I do have a mother and father, Ma doing the cooking and Da earning the money to keep the three of us. So why can't I be happy Ma's come home?

Living with Ma is like being on a roller coaster, a ride that started way back in grade one when she took to the rum. Her at the controls and me hogtied three cars back.

I'm not blind; I can see she really means to stop drinking. But she's promised to quit plenty of times before. Sooner or later something sets her off, out comes the bottle, and everything falls apart again. Sometimes slow, sometimes fast. Either way, me and Da left to pick up the pieces and go on as if nothing happened.

When I was little, I used to creep around the house watching her, spying on her from behind the couch, trying to be a perfect daughter so I wouldn't get her going. Dead certain that if only I paid more attention, I'd figure out what I was doing wrong. Even after she poured the first shot of rum, I'd make tea for her just the way she likes it, in the hopes she'd give me a hug and pour the rest of the bottle down the sink. How pathetic was that.

I thought I'd grown up the last few months, gotten mature so I wouldn't mind what she does. Lying to yourself is pathetic, too.

I've never been on an actual roller coaster because fairs and circuses don't come this way. But I've watched them on TV. The catch is, once they're moving, you can't climb off. Game over until the end of the ride.

What's the end of the ride for me? When I finish high school, shake the barrens—and Ma—off my boots, and head south?

I'm just a kid and not doing so hot. That's a lot of years to spend screaming your head off.

THIRTEEN

'pred·a·tors

Lunchtime Thursday I'm sitting next to Hector in the cafeteria, nose buried in my book. LaVaughn's describing the apartment where she babysits, its plugged sink and garbage and goo, you can just about smell it—when a plate smashes on the floor right behind Hector. The noise rips through me. I drop the book and whip around in my chair.

It was Mel's plate. An orange slime of spaghetti is spattered on the concrete floor, although she managed to jump back so it didn't splash her sneakers.

She looks right foolish. "Sorry," she mutters.

Mel, saying she's sorry? "If you ask at the counter, they'll send someone with a mop," I say, wondering about this generosity of spirit gig—Mel not exactly being my friend.

She stumbles off in the direction of the counter. "Keep your chair right where it is, Hector," I add. "You're some lucky she missed you."

He's frowning at Mel's back. "Waste of good spaghetti."

I turn around in my chair again. My sandwich is still sitting on the wax paper, but my book's not there. I give my head a little shake. Of course it's there, it's got to be. I push the sandwich around, then I check my lap and the floor.

"Hector," I say, panicking, "do you see my book?"

"The one you were reading?"

"Yeah, the one I was reading."

He shoves his books around and peers under the table. "Nope," he says. "Where was it?"

"Right in front of me—it can't be gone!"

Mel's behind us again, along with the janitor carrying a pail and mop. Mel stands back, watching the cleanup. But all of a sudden she shoots a quick look my way, a look loaded with malice and glee.

She didn't steal my book, she couldn't have.

With a sick lurch in my stomach, I realize she was the diversion. One of the other Shrikes stole it. Tate, I bet.

I surge to my feet. "Give me back my book!"

"Book? Do you see me with a book?" Mel spreads her hands, which are empty, her smile stretching clear to her ears.

"Has Tate got it?" I look around, frantic. "Did anyone see Tate steal my book?"

The other kids look away. No one's going to squeal on Tate Cody.

"Watch my sandwich," I say to Hector and rush out of the canteen. Up and down the halls, past the lockers, push open the gym door, no Tate. When I go outside, shivering because I'm only wearing a T-shirt, I see her by the school bus, dragging on a cigarette.

I march right up to her. "I want my book back."

"Book?" she says. "What book?"

"Don't, Tate."

My voice is a stranger's. Her eyes narrow. "Lotta fuss over a lousy book," she says.

No room in her jacket pockets for the book, and her jeans are too tight for anything but Tate. She must have hidden it in her locker.

"I'm going straight to the principal."

"Go ahead. But you can kiss your cats good-bye."

My gut plummets. I never told Ma about keeping the cats indoors—I was too busy thinking about stupid roller coasters. "Anything happens to my cats, I'll set Corporal Deakins on you!"

She blows a smoke ring in my face. "I'm real scared."

"You'd better be. You can't sneeze in Ratchet without the whole street reporting you're down with pneumonia. If you touch the cats, I'd have witnesses, and witnesses are what policemen go for."

She pokes me in the chest; her eyes have gone empty. "Travis Keating's a friend of yours. You wouldn't want him getting beat up, would you?"

Ice in my gut now. "By you and who else?"

"Hud Quinn hates Travis. Everyone knows that."

"Hud goes his own way."

"Hud has secrets, same as the rest of us—and I know what some of them are."

I'm caught in a snare; the more I struggle, the tighter it gets. "You leave Travis out of this," I say, but even to myself, I don't sound convincing. Way back in April, when Travis punched Mel, Tate told him he'd be sorry. She's waited this long to get her revenge.

She smiles, a smile as empty as her eyes. "You can have your book back and save yourself a whole lot of grief. You know the price. Seventy bucks. By tomorrow."

"I already forked out enough to replace your camera!" I take a step forward, my fists clenched.

She says, "Don't even think it—Mel could make hamburger out of you."

A trickle of sense seeps through the anger. But it's only a trickle. "You should read that book, Tate, you might learn a thing or two. About a girl who lives in a slum and she's got no dad, but she stays decent. Decent's harder than what you do. You're nothing but a slime-livered coward."

I turn on my heel and march back into the building. Why do I feel I could take on ten Tates when my book's still missing?

In the cafeteria, Hector's chowing down on cookies his mother baked. I sit beside him. I'm breathing hard and my appetite's flown out the window.

"Tate stole my book," I say. "Seventy bucks and it's mine."

"Seventy dollars for a *book*?"

What will I do without LaVaughn? She's like the girlfriend I never had. But I can't risk Travis getting beat up.

Somehow I get through the afternoon. Once everyone is off the bus except me and Travis, I sit down next to him. "No sense in you coming to my place for reading today, because Tate stole my book. She'll give it back—cash only."

"Don't you dare pay her!"

"If I don't, she threatened to set Hud on you."

"As long as I stick around with the guys, I'm safe enough. Can't you get the book back any other way?"

"Stage a midnight raid on Tate's locker?"

Travis frowns. "Too bad Hud's not on our side," he says. "I bet he could get it back."

"Hud as your best buddy?" I'm the closest to smiling that I've been all day. "Like that's going to happen. Travis, you watch out for him."

He nods as the bus pulls up at my driveway. "I'll let you know if I think of anything."

When I go in the house, Ma's standing at the sink listening to fiddle music on the radio, a coffee mug in her hand. Tansy and Rogue are playing with her laces.

"Ma, I don't let the cats outdoors. Scared to. You be careful to keep them in, okay? Da and me have been locking the front door. Just in case."

"Sure," she says, a little too casual for my liking. "No reading today?"

"Nope. What's for supper?"

"Meatloaf." Gently she nudges Rogue with the toe of her sneaker. "Give over, buddy, I won't have any laces left. Want to peel some carrots, Prinny?"

Even the cats are happy Ma's home.

"Thought I'd go out on the barrens."

Shrugging, Ma turns to look out the window. "Go ahead."

I tromp along the caribou trail, guilt dogging my heels. Ma's likely lonely with me and Da gone all day. Here I am telling Tate to act decent and I can't even peel a few carrots. My footsteps slow. I could go back. It's not too late.

The sun's warm for mid-May. I breathe in juniper and crowberry. A fox sparrow's singing in the alders, a clear sign of spring. His voice is like the flute Phoebe Sugden plays at the talent shows; the wonder of his song goes right through me. Words start dancing in my head, and somehow they hitch themselves to LaVaughn's short lines.

I sit down on the nearest rock. Say the words out loud. Picture the lines in my head, change them around, and hope no one's out here listening to me. This is what I end up with:

> "*Among the catkins*
> *a fox sparrow sings, clear*
> *as a flute, his feathers*
> *redder than the vixen's fur,*
> *his song pure joy.*"

What's with me talking in short lines like LaVaughn, spouting poetry on the barrens?

I know one thing. I don't want to go home.

At the den, I settle myself downwind and wait. Almost as though the poem made it happen, the vixen crawls onto the mound and stretches luxuriously. She's molting. She sniffs an old bone, then lies on her belly, basking in the sun, her black nose tasting the air, whiskers quivering.

Her ears twitch as the male fox comes over the rise, dragging a dead rabbit, blood along its jaw. She wags her tail, its white tip brushing the dirt, and the two of them touch noses before the male disappears into the den, tugging the rabbit behind him.

Although my feet are cold in my rubber boots, I stay put until the vixen goes back into the den. I feel sorry for rabbits because they're always trying to sniff out danger before it sinks claws and teeth into them.

I've warned Ma about the cats. I've warned Travis about Hud. Damage control. That's all I've been doing since the camera plopped in the toilet. That, and lying to Tate about money. The uncomplicated use of *lie*.

I'm giving up on *naïve*. If I pay for the frigging camera, the whole $150, Tate won't stop there. I'd be like a school of herring—dip your net in anytime.

I just wish I wasn't so scared of her. Jumpier than any rabbit.

I set the table for Ma when I get home, starting a conversation about the herbs that taste good in meatloaf and whether oatmeal makes it less soggy. Girl stuff. She says, "We'll go shopping tomorrow night, Prinny. Mrs. Dooks's brother isn't doing so good. There'll be a funeral soon enough, and your jacket's a disgrace."

"Sneakers, too?"

"We'll see. I'll check the flyers before we go."

By morning, Travis hasn't come up with any brilliant ideas of how to get my book back, although he says he's still working on it.

"You're not planning on paying Tate, are you?"

"Dunno yet."

"She'll milk you dry." He punches me lightly on the arm. "Stick to your guns—you can do it."

At recess, feeling like a rabbit facing fifty foxes, I force myself to walk over to Tate. "You can keep the book," I say. "I can't lay my hands on seven dollars, let alone seventy."

"Guess I'll give the book back to you," Tate says, and for a split second I think she's read it and it's changed her the way it's changing me. "Page by page."

"You mean you'll tear the book up?" I'm barely whispering, the thought's so painful.

"It's only paper."

Paper. With a whole bunch of black marks on it that were starting to make sense of my life. But if the fox could eat the fox sparrow, it would. Singing or no singing.

"There'll be other consequences," Tate says. "From all your reading, I bet you know what that word means."

The foxes creep closer. The rabbit shivers and shakes. "I'm not paying you one more penny," I say.

It almost sounds like I mean it.

FOURTEEN

'in·ter·lude

Friday night Ma and me go shopping. In Walmart my eyes light right away on a lime-green jacket. Pursing her lips, Ma says, "Not a good color for you, Prinny," and she's right. She searches along the rack and pulls out a cherry-red jacket with slash pockets. It looks great on me; then we find sneakers with cool laces.

In Violet's Boutique I try on a pair of embroidered jeans, half-price. Ma nods in approval. All this takes my mind off Tate and LaVaughn, and for once things are easy between Ma and me; she's a born shopper.

As we leave Violet's, Ma says, "Lordy, there's Hector's mother. She's so proper she makes me feel I'm tipsy when I'm stone-cold sober. I'll run to the Ladies—she'd never use a public washroom."

"I'll wait here," I say. "No rush."

Across the mall is the teacher's supply store, rigged up to look like a toy store from the outside. I went in there once. Verb charts, bulletin boards, racks and racks of workbooks about phonics, math skills, and language arts.

I wouldn't be so scared of it now.

I'm drifting off, playing some more with my poem about the fox sparrow, when two people come out of the supply store. My cousin Hud, wearing his black hockey jacket and jeans with the knees out. His little sister Fleur is beside him. Her pink trousers are too short; her jacket, also pink, could do with a trip to the Laundromat. She's holding a plastic bag as carefully as if it contains a million dollars.

Hud Quinn shopping with his sister on a Friday night?

Fleur stops, takes a big yellow box of crayons out of the bag, and opens the box, gazing into it as if she can't quite believe how lucky she is. She pulls out a thick red crayon. Then she tips the box sideways to get at another one. The crayons slide out, graceful as a waterfall, and tumble to the floor. She grabs Hud by the leg.

My feet dig into the floor; my muscles tense. Hud's not going to swipe that little kid. Not while I'm around.

Hud stoops, his bare knees poking out of his jeans, and starts picking up crayons, one by one. The light falls across his cheek, where high over the bone a purple bruise curves like a crescent moon. He didn't have that bruise on the bus after school; I'd have noticed.

Fleur holds out the empty box, chattering away to him. As he tucks the first crayons in and adjusts her hand to hold the box upright, Hud answers her. She hunkers down, stuffing a green crayon in the box with her free hand, still talking. He smiles. A creaky smile, like a gate that's hardly ever opened.

Somehow I don't think he'd want me watching him. I turn my back and hurry to the washroom. Ma's coming out, so I steer her toward the doors at the far end of the mall, yakking on about my new jacket, storing that picture of Hud and Fleur in the corner of my brain where I keep stuff I can't possibly explain.

After we meet up with Da at Home Hardware, we all go for Chinese food. The whole time we're there, Ma's lit up, like she's happy.

When Ma's happy, so is Da. Nothing complicated about that.

I do my best to forget about the bruise on Hud's cheek.

Six a.m. Da and me are heading out of Fiddlers Cove in *Wilma Marie*, the waves banging against the fiberglass prow, *whomp, whomp, whomp,* gulls screaming overhead in the hopes bait will be tossed overboard.

I'm wearing my thickest socks inside my rubber boots, with oilskins over my parka. The sky's empty of clouds, gold spilling over the sea at the horizon.

The markers for our pots are painted the green of shamrocks; Da's that proud of his Irish ancestors. I pick up the gaff—a long wooden pole with a metal hook on one end—and snag the first line. Da fits it over the winch and up comes the pot, streaming water. He swings it over the side of the boat. I take out the lobster. No need to measure, it's easy a pound and a half. Da snaps the blue rubber bands over its claws, I throw it in the bucket, and while Da pitches the chewed bait overboard along with a cluster of sea urchins, I stick a fresh chunk of herring on the nail in the trap.

I love the way we work together, no hitches like there are with Ma. As Da dumps the pot back in the sea,

gulls swoop on wings
made of feathers and light.

I can see the words in my head—I'm surprised I didn't say them out loud. Can two lines be a poem? Da shoves the throttle forward and we chug to the next marker.

His line of pots is inside the reef we call Knuckle-bones. Reefs edge the shore here for miles: Hare's Ears, Hook Nose, Scroggins, and Push Through. Even at high tide, the sea slops and gurgles around exposed rocks, kelp swaying back and forth; but it's the under-water spines of the reef that are so treacherous, sharp enough to rip the keel from your boat.

The second trap's empty; Da baits it again. But in the third one, the lobster's a keeper. By the time we come to the last trap, the sun's warm on our backs and we've got ourselves a good haul. We can see the other boats rocking on the swell; Da waves to them as we pass. As we thread between the rocks at the entrance to the cove, we have our usual argument.

"I think you should call *Wilma Marie* an outport boat," I say. "Sounds nicer."

"Speedboat's good enough for me," Da says. Then we grin at each other.

I sit quiet, watching the lobster clamber over each other in the plastic crate. We moor *Wilma Marie* at the wharf, next to the little wooden dory that Da built. By noon, we're back home. A hot shower does wonders. So does the pea soup with doughboys that Ma serves for lunch. Rayleen would give Ma full points for that soup.

Just as I finish the dishes, Travis arrives at the door. I invite him in. "Can't stay," he says, standing on the step. "We ordered your lemonade book last night, Dad and me, on the Internet. It'll take a week or ten days to get here. So now you can tell Tate to go stuff herself."

"I already did. You mean—"

"You did? Good for you, Prinny! That was really brave."

I'm blushing. "You can buy books online?" I say. "But how much will it cost? 'Cause I'll pay for it."

He looks uncomfortable. "I told Dad what happened. He wants to buy it for you."

If people are mean to me, I can be lippy as a Whiskey Jack. But when they're nice, I'm right fuddled. I shuffle my feet in my old pink slippers. "Thanks... tell your dad thanks, too."

"I'll bring the book over as soon as it arrives. See you."

He runs down the driveway. Although he's likely off to visit Laice, not even that can make me feel bad. Ten days max and I'll find out what's happening to LaVaughn.

Maybe these poems—although poems is too fancy a word—keep flying into my head because I miss LaVaughn. Miss her something awful. I don't write them down. Trying to put them on paper might turn them into...into...as I step back inside the porch, the words sort themselves around a picture I've seen a hundred times.

Starlings landing on fresh snow—
don't tap the window!
They'll swirl away—up
up into the sky—

and whoever heard of a poet who can't read? Short lines. That's what I'll call them. My short lines.

After lobstering, I usually take a nap in the afternoon. But today I'm antsy as a rabbit that's trying to outwit a fox. So I shove my water bottle in my pocket, hike the barrens, and sit by the den for an hour or so, not thinking about much of anything, gradually feeling more and more peaceful. God's a big mystery to me. Times he seems like Uncle Doyle—terrifying, powerful, downright mean to His only Son. But out here He surrounds me. Still as granite, huge as the sky, beckoning like the faraway Blue Hills.

I'm almost asleep when two blunt, black-furred noses poke out of the hole: pups, testing the air. They back off, I hear squealing inside, then the vixen comes out to lie in the sun.

When she goes back down the hole, I get up real quiet, stretch, and pick my way across the barrens to the dirt road that leads from Gulley Cove. Lots of times Travis and me came this way, along the cliffs, while we were feeding the cats.

I'll have to write a note to Dr. Keating, thanking him for my book. It was nice of him to pay for it.

A book that's more than a book.

And a friend who thinks I'm brave.

FIFTEEN

first 'cous·in

Far below, the surf is sighing against the cliffs—long sighs, one after another. Then, all of a sudden, my ears feel like fox ears, straining to catch sounds on the wind. Someone's screaming. High-pitched. A girl. I start to run, racing up the hill past Abe Murphy's, toward Ratchet and the other houses.

Three people in the middle of the dirt road, an ATV parked by the ditch.

Hud's got Travis down, kicking him. Travis is trying to shield his face and grab hold of Hud's leg at the same time. Laice is shrieking as she tugs Hud's jacket and pounds on his back with her fists; she's got to be hurting him.

I'm onto them fast. I kick Hud vicious-hard in the back of the knee, watch it buckle and him stagger, and kick him again. Laice lands another punch, giving me time to unscrew the lid of my water bottle, duck under his arm, and fling the water full in his face. He jerks backward, scrubbing at his eyes, snarling a cussword.

Travis rolls out of reach of Hud's boots. I squawk, "I'll set Aunt Ida on you, Hud Quinn! You want her telling your da what you're up to?" This being the worst threat I can think of.

"*Prinny*?" Hud says, his face changing from crazed to something approaching normal. Water's trickling down his cheeks like tears. Which is a laugh. I figure Hud forgot how to cry a long time ago, and who can blame him?

The bruise on his cheek is darker than it was yesterday.

"Tate put you up to this?" I say, gasping for air.

"Tate? What are you talking about?"

"She's the one who told you to beat up Travis—right?"

"I got no truck with the likes of Tate Cody."

Relief can feel like having your sins forgiven. "Keep it that way, okay?"

"Don't you go giving me orders!"

Laice is still punching him, not realizing the fight's over. Hud swats at her absently, as if she's a moose fly. Caught off-guard, she tumbles top over scrapers on the road. Travis is lurching to his feet, favoring one leg.

"The cops got your number, Hud," I say, "you forgetting that? You better vamoose."

Laice has rolled over and scrambled to her feet.

As she puts her head down to charge Hud, Travis latches onto her elbow, hauling her sideways. She screeches, "Let go!"

Hud lands a swift jab on Travis's shoulder that makes him totter. He bumps into Laice, and nearly sends her flying again. Then Hud lopes over to his ATV. The engine growls and off he goes.

Laice lets out her breath in a loud *whoooof*. Her eyes are the blue you see at the edge of flames. Gripping Travis's sleeve, her voice rough, she says, "Did he hurt you?"

His jacket and face are streaked with dirt. A cut over his eyebrow has daubed blood on his forehead; he's rubbing his hip. Not meeting her gaze, he shakes off her hand. "I'm fine. Thanks. I gotta go."

His fists thrust deep in his pockets, his shoulders hunched, he limps away.

Laice takes a couple of steps after him, stops, takes another step, and stops again. "What's eating him?" she says blankly.

"Leave him be," I say. "He'll get over it."

"Is he mad at me? What did I do?"

"Guys don't like being rescued by girls. They're supposed to do any rescuing that needs doing."

"Oh," says Laice.

"Plus they're not supposed to need rescuing."

"That's stupid! Hud's way bigger than Travis."

"I didn't say it had anything to do with common sense."

She's staring at me as if she's never seen me before. She says slowly, "You got Hud's attention in a hurry."

"You didn't do so bad yourself—you pack a mean punch."

Suddenly we're grinning at each other.

She giggles. "You should have seen the look on Hud's face when you kicked him. That was a dirty trick, aiming for his knee."

"Looked to me like you've been clobbering Halifax bullies every day of your life."

Now we're both giggling. "Girl power!" Laice cries, grabs me by the sleeve, and whirls me in a circle. We whoop and holler like a couple of lunatics. Then we collapse in a heap on the road.

Laice fumbles in her pocket. "Gran made coconut drops—would you like one?" She unwraps the foil package. The cookies are crushed, crumbs instead of drops, and for some reason this sets us off again.

We crunch coconut between our teeth, licking raspberry jam from our fingers. "Some good," I say. "Thanks."

She sobers. "I'm the one who should be saying thanks. I couldn't stop Hud on my own—he was scary."

"That's okay." I stand up. "I'd better be going."

"Will you come to my place one day after school?"

You ever hear someone say something and in the same moment you're convinced they couldn't possibly have said it?

"I—I'd like to."

"How about Monday? I could loan you some books, now that you're into reading."

She starts telling me about a fantasy novel she was given for Christmas—dragons and forests and an enchanted castle. I have to say, it does sound exciting. First thing you know, we're at my driveway.

She says, talking fast, "I'm sorry I was mean to you that day on the barrens, and at the rink. I hated being here, but I shouldn't have taken it out on you. I really am sorry...bye for now, Prinny."

"Bye," I say to her back because she's already running down the road. I feel like I'm singing inside, like I'm still whirling in a circle arm in arm with Laice. She and me just might become friends. Imagine that!

Wonder how Hud would feel if I thanked him?

Wonder if his dad gave him the bruise on his cheek and he was just passing it along?

SIXTEEN

'cour·age

Laice's bedroom is fit for a princess. The carpet's off-white; the windows have ruffled pink gingham curtains, and blinds with a silk fringe and a crocheted ring for pulling them down. Framed pictures on the wall, a TV and DVD player parked in a white cabinet, a stereo system on the bookshelves. Which also have books on them, enough books to make you run for cover.

The closet's partway open. Racks of clothes, waiting for Laice to choose what to wear.

My own room slinks into my head. Bare. Not just bare, threadbare. An old bathmat beside the bed so my feet don't hit the linoleum first thing. A quilt, hand stitched by Ma's grandmother on a bed that doesn't even have a headboard for all that I've been bugging Da to make me one. I tacked a couple of cat pictures on the wall from a calendar Da was going to throw away. Rogue's been using one leg of the dresser for a scratching post.

It's easy to see Laice takes her room for granted.

But then, her parents can afford to go on a cruise. They could sail twice around the world, by the looks of it.

Laice's grandmother taps on the door. "I brought you girls a lunch," she says, and puts down a tray set with juice glasses, coconut drops, and gooey brownies that make my mouth water. Napkins as well, printed with little pink flowers.

After she goes out, we sit on the bed with its frilly pillow shams; I've seen them in the catalogue, never figured there was much point to them. When Laice passes the plate of brownies, I take one. Laice is the city girl and I'm the outport kid, that's the way of it; me being excited all day about coming here seems like plain foolishness now.

"Are you all right?" Laice says.

I say the first thing that comes into my head. "Your mother and father enjoying their cruise?"

The brownie jerks in her hand. She sets it down carefully on the plate. "They're having a wonderful time."

Now I feel it's my turn to say, *You all right?* Are there rules with girlfriends for what you can say and what you can't? I lick icing from between my teeth. "You own a ton of books."

"Gran rations the TV. Besides, I like reading," she says with a touch of defiance. She wipes her fingers on a napkin before taking a paperback from the top shelf. "You spend a lot of time outdoors, Prinny. You'd like this book."

Silverwing it's called, with a bat on the cover. I open it. Print dense on every page and lines all the way to the far edge. Panic rises, same as when Mrs. Dooks is waiting for me to read about the perfect dog Ben on Monday afternoons.

Today's Monday. "Mrs. Dooks's brother died on Saturday," I say, laying the book on the bed. "You going to the visitation? It's tomorrow night at the funeral parlor in town."

"Gran said we were. I've never been to a funeral parlor."

"Never?"

"Is there a coffin?"

"Yeah, but it's not so bad. People line up to pay their respects, then they stand around and talk. Even if the coffin's open, the person in it doesn't look dead. More like a wax doll."

Although I truly meant to reassure her, her eyes are stretched as wide as they'll go. "The lid up? Like in a horror movie? I'm not going!"

"I'll be there—and Travis."

"I don't care!"

I've blown it. "You want to read the first page or two of the bat book? Out loud?"

"Okay," she says, seizes the book, and buries her nose in it. At the start she reads too fast, but gradually she gets into the rhythm of it; and first thing you know I'm hooked, gone, off with Shade and Chinook hunting tiger moths in the dark. Shade, whose nickname is Runt and who's used to being ignored…

She reads five or six pages. Then she puts the book down. We smile at each other, me chin-deep in relief; the pink pillow shams don't matter at all.

"Thanks," I say. "That's awesome."

Last fall Mrs. Dooks made me read a story about a girl called Gladys who had two pet mice, Cuddles and Pansy—a story so cute it was enough to curdle your stomach. I never realized a book about animals could be told differently, from the inside, as if you're the bat. Do you think anyone's written about foxes that way?

The clock radio by Laice's bed says quarter of five. "I'd better go. We eat early because of Da lobstering." I wrestle my courage to the ground. "My bedroom's not fancy like this, but maybe sometime you could come to my place and meet the cats. Tansy and Rogue."

"I love cats." A shadow crosses her face. "My mum's allergic to them, so I can't have one. Let's do it soon."

Easy as pie. I walk home in a daze. I've got me a

girlfriend, my very first one, and it doesn't seem to matter that her parents are on a world cruise or that she's pretty as a picture.

My cup runneth over. First time I've come close to understanding what that means.

Next morning on the bus, Travis is still in a grump, ignoring me and Laice as if we're the ones who had him down in the dirt kicking the tar out of him. Laice sits next to me, although she doesn't have much to say for herself.

At lunchtime I arrive in the cafeteria ahead of her; I make sure there's an empty seat next to me, and unwrap my sandwich. Just as I notice the noise dying down, I see the reason why—Tate's marching toward me, girl on a mission. She takes a plastic bag from behind her back, opens it, tips it upside down over my plate, and shakes it.

An avalanche of paper scraps settles over my egg-salad sandwich. I see *ockroac* written on one scrap, *aVaug* on another.

I'm on my feet before I know it. Grabbing a handful of paper, I fling it in her face. It drifts over her shoulders like confetti. "You're pathetic, you know that?" I scream, and the words echo the length of the room because everyone's gone silent.

Tate snaps her fist into my belly. I yelp with pain,

fill both hands with bits of paper, and jam them in her face, blinding her.

"You don't have the guts to read that book—alls you can do is rip it to shreds!"

From the corner of one eye, I see Mel coming on the run; from the corner of the other, Travis rushing to the rescue, Cole, Buck, and Stevie on his heels. Even Hector's on his feet, with Laice fast overtaking Stevie. Terror and laughter are all mixed up in my chest—laughter because it took LaVaughn to make me find *my* guts, terror because Mel's going to grind my face into the floor before anyone can stop her.

Mr. Marsden shouts, "Girls! Girls! Prinny, sit down. Tate, go straight back to your table."

Huffing, he stops by my chair. "Hector, get a broom to sweep up the mess. We cannot have incidents like this in the cafeteria. You and Prinny are on detention, Tate. Hector, the broom."

Hector winks at me and shuffles off. Mel glares at Travis, who glares right back. As nervous laughter ripples around the cafeteria, Mr. Marsden does his share of glaring. The kids start talking again, and under cover of the noise Tate says, "Won't always be a teacher around, Prinny—you better watch your back." Then she and Mel return to their table.

My knees feel like they're made of Jello. I latch onto my chair and fall into the seat. After Mr. Marsden gives a couple of *harrumphs*, he walks away. The hems of his trousers are frayed.

Detention means you stay indoors at recess. No problem.

I sift through the papers on my plate, sorting whole words, parts of words, even phrases where the pieces are big enough. That's the way I read, words separate from sense. No clue as to the whole.

It's the way I used to read.

I screamed insults at Tate in front of the whole school. Detective shows on TV call that kind of behavior *temporary insanity*.

SEVENTEEN

wake

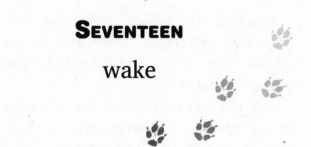

The funeral parlor's warm and the coffin's open. First person I see is Father Gogan in his long black robe. His crucifix is tipped forward over his belly, giving Jesus a fine view of a pair of scuffed black shoes.

Ma hasn't been anywhere public like this for months. At least, not sober. Her fingers are digging into my shoulder through my navy-blue sweater. Da says, "There's Mrs. Dooks, Wilma. We'll speak to her first."

Mrs. Dooks looks smaller here than in the classroom. We say all the expected things, and she says the expected things back. Freaks me out, feeling sorry for Mrs. Dooks.

Afterward, we view her brother Albert in his coffin. Not even the undertaker's been able to make Albert look cheerful.

I always feel relieved when that part's over. But then Aunt Ida cuts through the crowd and parks herself in front of Ma. "I'm surprised to see *you* here, Wilma," she says in a voice that reaches every corner of the room.

Aunt Sebina bustles up, Uncle Ralph in her wake. "Now, Ida," she scolds, "leave well enough alone. You look good, Wilma, and I'm right pleased to see you out and about."

Aunt Ida opens her mouth, Da steps hard on her toe, and whatever she was going to say changes into a gasp of outrage. Da says calmly, "Nice to see you, Sebina. Ralph, this gotta be the best lobster season in five years. You making a dollar?"

They're off, and as Aunt Sebina gabbles on about spring-cleaning, Aunt Ida gives a loud sniff and stalks away.

Next thing you know, Father Gogan has joined us. "Wilma," he says heavily, "it's a long time since I've seen you."

Ma flushes scarlet. Da stiffens. "You're seeing her now," he says.

Father Gogan directs his you-disappoint-me-greatly-but-I'll-do-my-best-to-bear-it look on Ma. "Confession, Wilma," he says. "Confession's the next step—so that you can receive the sacrament in a state of grace."

Da says, "To quit drinking, seems to me, is grace enough for anyone."

Father Gogan draws himself to his full height, which is several inches shorter than Da's. "Now, Thomas, you look after your lobster traps and allow me to look after Wilma's immortal soul."

"I'm looking after my marriage, that's what I'm doing," Da says. "Now, if you'll excuse us..." and he leads us across the room to where Mr. and Mrs. Baldwin are standing, Mr. Baldwin minus the soup can he spits into when he chews tobacco. Slowly the buzz of conversation picks up.

Da looks like he just pulled a five-pounder out of the pot. Normally by now he'd be off in the corner with his fishing buddies, talking quotas and riptides. Tonight he's sticking so close to Ma that I'm jealous.

Jealous. Of my own mother.

She's eyeing the door as if she'd like to make a run for it.

Mattie and Starald arrive, Laice trailing behind them. Laice looks snooty, which I'm beginning to understand means she's scared. They go straight over to Mrs. Dooks, Laice not even noticing me standing there, then they approach the coffin. By now, Mattie's gripping Laice by the elbow. Laice is white-faced. She stares blankly at Albert, glances up, and her whole face brightens.

Dr. Keating's standing by the door signing the guestbook. He passes the pen to Travis. As Mattie and Starald walk over to join us, Laice pulls free and hurries toward Travis.

Dr. Keating says something to Laice, smiling at her. Travis puts the pen down, then barges past her to the far corner of the room where Stevie and Buck are standing in their St. Fabien Furies jackets.

Laice looks like he just slapped her in the face. Dr. Keating pats her on the shoulder; from the way he's frowning, Travis is in for it. But I'm not waiting for Dr. Keating. I steam across the room toward those hockey jackets, and when I reach them, I slice Travis away from his buddies like he's a sheep and I'm one of those black-and-white dogs I've seen on TV. Remembering to keep my voice low, a miracle in itself, I say, "Laice thinks you're worth diddly because you let Hud knock you down."

Travis chews on his lip, looking so unhappy I'm almost sorry for him. "She told you that?"

"No. She didn't. I made it up. But that's what you think she thinks."

Now he looks mad. "Quit it, Prinny."

"It's one thing to be half Hud's size. Another to act like you've got half his brain."

"I'm way smarter than him!"

"Yeah? Then you go right back to Laice and apologize, and you be nice to her from now on."

I can't believe *(a)* that I'm having a fight with Travis in the funeral parlor and *(b)* that I'm pushing him at Laice. Wakes are usually dull as dumplings.

Da's looking for me. "I have to go," I say. "Smarten up, Travis Keating, and be glad your friends don't stand around watching Hud pound on you."

He says in a strangled voice, "It's nice to see your mum here, Prinny," and I realize that's why I can't help liking the guy—he understands what a big deal it is, Ma being sober.

Funeral parlors must remind him of his own mum. I give his shoulder a jab, figuring if I hugged him he'd melt with mortification and I might start to bawl. Then I hurry back to Da and Ma, wishing I had the chance to talk to Laice. Ma looks downright jittery, like she'd give her soul for a drink. My stomach twists in a knot.

Da says, "Ready, Prinny?" and what can I say but *yes*?

We troop outside to the truck and drive home, Ma sitting in the window seat, gazing out, me in the little cab behind. While the silence of the barrens is as near to paradise as I'm likely to get, this silence, full of things no one's saying, drives me nuts.

"Aunt Ida's your sister, Ma, and Father Gogan is supposed to be joyful in the Lord," I say. "I wouldn't want to be stranded on Knucklebones with either one of them."

Da snorts with laughter. Ma says, like she's talking to the spruce trees, "Don't try fixing things for me, Prinny. Any fixing to be done, I'll do it."

So she *can* still hurt me.

Da says, "Now, Wilma—"

"And don't you start, neither!"

She's being so unfair I'm just about choking. I open my mouth to let the words spill out, but Da's frowning at me in the rearview mirror, shaking his head, so I sink back in my seat. He lets her walk all over him.

All over me, as well.

I'm in one of the cubicles in the girls' washroom at noon hour, a place where I used to feel safe. Now I'm watching the floor for three pairs of sneakers.

Laice and Travis have made up, and Laice gave me a big smile on the bus. I'm in hopes she'll take over reading to me after school, because she likes the same kind of books I do. Ma didn't get my breakfast this morning, but I was okay with not laying eyes on her before I left, forgiveness not being as easy as it cracks up to be.

A couple of other girls come into the washroom. Joan Bidson says, "If Laice thinks she can hang around with Prinny Murphy and me at the same time, she can think again."

Nicole, the lawyer's daughter, says, "An ultimatum?"

"Straight choice. Prinny or me."

Nicole giggles. "What if she chooses Prinny?"

"If she's that much of a dork, why would I want her for a friend?"

Water runs in the sink. Joan says, "Buck told Caitlin that Travis doesn't like the way Laice nags at him. Probably he'll dump her."

As Nicole giggles again, they clatter out the door. I stay put, rubbing my cold hands on my knees. I don't think Travis is about to dump Laice. After she hears Joan's ultimatum, she might dump me, though. Thing is, I don't really trust her. The laughter that held us together on the Gulley Cove road was a great start. But I'm scared friendship is like a rubber band—stretch it and it snaps.

There's nothing like a hard toilet seat for foisting honesty on you. It isn't Laice I don't trust. It's me. Deep down, I don't believe I'm worth having a friendship with. Now that Laice and Travis are buddy-buddy again, she won't have the time of day for me.

After school, Mattie and Starald pick Laice up in their car, so I don't get to talk to her, or ask her about reading. I walk up our driveway, trying not to drag my feet. The truck's gone, so Da's not home. The kitchen's empty, no signs of supper or of Ma. Maybe she's off with Da.

I'm walking down the hall when a creepy feeling on the back of my neck warns me I'm not alone in the house. I peer into Da's bedroom. Ma's in bed, covers pulled up to her chin, her eyes shut. She looks right puny. Sitting on the dresser, in plain view, is one of the bottles from the back closet. It's three-quarters full.

She gives a tiny moan. I say, "What's up, Ma?" even though I know the answer.

Her eyes fly open. "Will you get supper, Prinny? I don't feel so good. Must be the flu."

"You've been drinking." That's when I remember the pills Dr. Keating put her on, the ones that make her sick if she drinks.

That's when we both hear Da in the porch, the *clunk, clunk* as he drops his boots on the mat, then the thump of his footsteps down the hall.

"Hide the bottle," Ma gasps. "*Please*, Prinny."

I've nearly reached the dresser when Da appears in the doorway. "What's the matter, Wilma? You sick?"

I stand between him and the bottle. Ma takes a deep, shuddery breath. "Tom," she says, "I had one drink. Only one, I swear. Last night, at the funeral parlor—I couldn't take it, I just couldn't take it, and today I needed a drink so bad…but the pills I'm on, they made me sick." Her laugh is the saddest thing I ever heard. "Serves me right, I guess."

I'm frozen to the floor. She told the truth.

Although I must say her one drink was a hefty one.

I'm not sure Da's even noticed I'm in the room. He says, "Now that you know they make you sick,

Wilma, alls you gotta do is keep taking them." But he's not just saying that. His face, as he walks toward the bed, sits down on it, and strokes her cheek with his big, rough hand, is saying, *I love you...I'll do whatever I can to help*.

I sneak out of the room. He must have seen me. But he didn't pay me no heed at all.

Eighteen

'vis·i·tors

End of the week comes as a big relief. I've been watching my back best I can, but so far Tate and her crew haven't made a move. Laice made my day Thursday when she invited me over to Mattie's again. I'm scared to ask her to our place. What if Ma quits taking the pills and we find her passed out on the floor?

Anyways—nope, I mean anyway—Laice read more of the bat book to me, then helped me stumble my way through a couple of paragraphs. She didn't make me feel one bit stupid. Do you think I might be lucky enough that her and me are becoming friends tied together with lobster line, which never snaps?

Once her parents come back from their cruise, she'll be gone from here. I can hardly bear to think of it.

I know one thing. After I finish the lemonade book, I plan to tackle the bat story, see if I can find room for me on pages where words go all the way from one side to the other. Then maybe I could try the book Mr. Roberts read about the guy who's broke and hungry and looking for his mother.

After school Friday, Aunt Ida's car is parked in the driveway. While I'm unlacing my sneakers in the porch, I eavesdrop.

"...as for that sweater you wore to the funeral parlor, it was too tight for a teenager, and you a married woman. I wonder at you, Wilma, I really do. Showing up at a wake bold as a jay, just like you aren't the talk of every community from here to Blandings. I can't believe—"

"I'm home, Ma!" I call, and sail into the kitchen in my cherry-red jacket.

Ma's backed against the table. Cornered and desperate is how she looks. "Prinny," she says, "I didn't realize it was that late. I gotta start supper, Ida. Tom gets home right hungry, and you said you had errands in St. Fabien—I wouldn't want to hold you up. I'm making a macaroni casserole, Sebina's recipe—"

"I'll find the macaroni, Ma," I say, and push past Aunt Ida.

Aunt Ida gives one of her sniffs. "You leave your manners at school, Prinny?"

"Ma's doing just fine."

"No respect for her elders, that girl of yours, Wilma. But then, what would you expect when she's hardly ever known—"

"Ma, why don't you put some water in the big pot?" I threw shredded paper at Tate, but I lack the nerve to pelt my aunt with macaroni.

"I don't know what the world's coming to," Aunt Ida says, and I wait for the next bit. "Going to hell in a handbasket, that's what."

Ma has the tap on full blast. I reach for the measuring cup, pour macaroni into it, and turn on the radio loud as I dare. It's the nautical channel.

...*Blandings to Salvage Shoals, winds south-south-west at twenty knots, decreasing to ten by nightfall*...

Aunt Ida thrusts her arms into her jacket. "I can tell when I'm not wanted," she says. Her heels rap across the linoleum. She slams the front door on her way out.

"I don't know what the world's coming to," I mimic. My laugh's edgy, even I can hear that. But Ma's leaning over the pot of water weeping like we're all going to hell, her shoulders quivering like someone's laying a whip to them.

I turn off the tap, unwrap her fingers from the handles of pot, and lower it into the sink. "It's okay, Ma, it's okay. She's the meanest woman the length of the shore—you mustn't listen to one word she says. Come on now, Da'll be home soon, needing his supper." She hauls in her breath; I can see she's trying. As if I'm the grown-up, I add, "You don't want

Da to see you crying. Go wash your face while I put the kettle on."

"Ida's like my dad," she says. "When I was a kid, anytime I was feeling okay about myself, or halfways happy, seemed like his job was to cut me down to size. Quick with his belt, he was always that. But him on a tirade—that's what I dreaded. Four words from him could peel the skin off your face."

"Worse than Uncle Doyle?"

"There's days I figure none of my family should've had kids," she says, pushing her hair back from her face as she stares out the window at who knows what. "Ida was smart that way."

I bump her aside with my hip. Then I dump the pot of water down the sink. "Enough tears in that water to salt a side of beef."

"I'll go wash my face," Ma says.

She looks so sad, so beaten, walking down the hall to the bathroom. I've been mean to her lots of times the last four or five years—did I remind her of Granddad? She's already told me I'm hard, same as Aunt Ida. Maybe meanness is inherited, like brown eyes. Aunt Ida got the meanness gene, and so did I.

Hud sure inherited Uncle Doyle's meanness. Just ask Travis. But if the way Hud picked up Fleur's crayons is anything to go by, he loves his little sister.

It's confusing when good and bad get mixed up.

One thing's clear enough, though. Ma shouldn't have had me—that's what she meant with her talk about no kids. No wonder I never had a sister.

I drag the cheese down the grater, make a white sauce the way Rayleen taught me, toss in pepper, the cheese, and a can of tuna because Da likes anything that comes from the sea, and stir it all together with the cooked macaroni. Bread crumbs on top with more grated cheese, and into the oven it goes.

Ma still hasn't come back to the kitchen.

We make it through supper, Da yawning because he's already been up more than twelve hours, Ma not saying much of anything. I do the dishes. I'm putting the last of the cutlery away when someone bangs on the door. Travis is on the step. I bring him in fast, shutting the door so the cats can't escape.

"Guess what?" he says. "Cloud's moved in with Abe, and your Aunt Sebina is taking Patches home with her this weekend."

"That's terrific!"

"We'll have to work really hard on taming Ghost."

Then he takes his hand from behind his back, offering me a brown padded envelope. It's heavier than I expected. "Is this what I think it is?"

"Open it and see."

It's the lemonade book, a brand new hardcover, the print crisp and tidy on the page. I turn to the beginning and read the first few words, trying not to cry.

Travis says gruffly, "Is it okay?"

"It's beautiful..."

"Came quicker than we thought."

"Now I've got it for the weekend." I remember the manners Aunt Ida says I don't have. "Would you like to stay a while? And, Travis, thanks."

"Gotta go—Dad and me are going shopping in St. Fabien."

"Thank him for me, will you?"

Once Travis has gone, I take out the box of note-paper Aunt Sebina gave me for Christmas two years ago. Yellow daisies parade across the top of each sheet. Using a new ballpoint, I write,

Dear Dr. Keating,

> *Thank you for my new book. I'm very grateful. I'll read some of it over the weekend. I hope you are keeping well.*

Prinny Murphy.

I had to look *grateful* up in the dictionary, took me a while to find it. I feel *great* and *full* of thanks, but it's not spelled that way.

I settle down early with the book, going over some of the pages I've already read, until I come to a place where LaVaughn's mom gets mad because LaVaughn's lagging in her homework. All of a sudden, emptiness fills the room.

I've never asked Laice if she misses her mother, off in a big white boat on the ocean. I know Travis still misses his. How can I miss mine when she lives in the same house?

Saturday morning and there's a good lop on, *Wilma Marie* bucking the waves, spray stinging my cheeks. The lobster are still going for the bait, and Da and me weave our jobs together tidy as twine. When I get home, Ma divvies up the housework with me; as long as we work in different rooms, we do okay. I throw the bathmat that's my bedside carpet into the washer, pin some new pictures on the wall by my bed, and put *Make Lemonade* on the shelf alongside my school books and my collection of shells, bones, and feathers.

Sunday afternoon when Laice phones, I ask her over. I put down the receiver, my heart thudding. Trying to sound casual, as though I have friends dropping in every day, I say, "Ma, Laice Hadden's coming for a visit—Mattie and Starald's grand-daughter from Nova Scotia."

For a moment Ma looks scared, causing me to see the kitchen through her eyes: the linoleum Da's never replaced, the grease spots over the stove, the tablecloth I should have thrown in the washer with the bathmat.

"I'll make tea," I say, "and there's double-chocolate Oreos in the cupboard. We can have it on a tray in my room." Then I rush off, brush my hair, change into my embroidered jeans, and plump up the pillows.

When the knock comes on the front door, I walk toward it like I'm on my way to the principal's office. But at the last minute Tansy and Rogue rush into the porch, so I have to pick them up before I open the door, then ask Laice to close it quick.

"They're adorable!" she says, taking Tansy in her arms, lifting her to her cheek, and letting Tansy's little pink nose sniff at her. She kicks off her sneakers and we're in the kitchen before you know it.

"Ma, this is Laice Hadden."

"Hi, Laice," Ma says. "Let me take your jacket...I'll make tea and bring it down to you."

First Rogue tries to climb up Laice's jeans, then he streaks down the hall as if the fox is on his tail. I lead the way to my room. Before she came, I pulled the blinds partway down and turned on the bedside lamp, so the room would look cozy. Laice scarcely looks at it. As she sits on the bed, Rogue jumps up and pounces on her knee while Tansy squirms to be let down.

Ma brings the tea in. Our best mugs on a tray cloth with lace around the edges, and I'm so grateful to Ma—that word again—that she gets the smile I usually keep for Da on *Wilma Marie*. She blinks—and smiles back.

After she's closed the door—I'm also grateful she understands this is a private visit—Laice says through a mouthful of chocolate, "Your mother's pretty. You're so lucky to have two cats. I wish I could have even one."

"Maybe your mother could take allergy pills when you go home," I say, hoping she'll tell me she's never going home.

"Maybe," she says and picks up her mug.

"You'll have to come to Abe's barn with me and Travis. This morning Rocky was all over us. We never saw Ghost, though—he's afraid of everything, including his own shadow."

"I'd like to do that."

"Joan Bidson said that if you hang around with me, she won't be your friend."

There. The words are out and it's too late to take them back.

"She's so full of being the mayor's daughter, she doesn't have room for a friend," Laice says, holding her cookie high so Rogue won't lick it. "Travis told me your book arrived."

We read for quite a while, her going first, me second. Then she asks me to read a couple of new pages on my own. Flustered, I bumble through the first paragraph. But the next paragraph is describing a photo of LaVaughn's dad, who she scarcely remembers. I want to know about him so bad that I clench my mind. Gradually the words smooth out, making phrases and sentences, making sense.

"Awesome," Laice says, grinning at me like I'm her prize pupil.

"I never knew I could do that!"

"We can practice another day. Tomorrow, perhaps."

"Are you really going to be an astrophysicist?"

"That was last month. I might be a costume designer for the movies instead." She strokes Rogue, who butts at her hand. "Or run a shelter for stray cats."

"If I can read, I can be anything I want..."

That's the thought—exciting and scary—that I take to bed with me.

Nineteen

'run·a·way

Monday first thing I run the lemonade book over to Laice's, because we agreed I'd read there after school. I don't want the book anywhere near the Shrikes.

Although it's sunny with a nice breeze, the marine forecast warned that a nor'easter is in the works for this afternoon. I believe the forecast more than this pretty blue sky—we often have days when the weather changes faster than you can change your socks.

Mrs. Dooks is back, but absentminded still. In remedial reading, the words settle themselves tidily on the page and I do okay, although the perfect dog Ben acts so noble it's sickening.

"Good," says Mrs. Dooks.

LaVaughn's a treat after Ben, so it's nearly five-thirty when I leave Laice's and race home, the nor'easter howling by now, rain beating against the shingles on the house. Da's truck isn't in the driveway; he must still be at the wharf. Likely the men have been hauling in their traps.

The door's locked, so I use my key. "Ma! What's for supper?"

She doesn't answer. The kitchen's empty. No Tansy purring in the rocking chair, no Rogue trotting up to attack my backpack. Beneath the whine of the gale and the rain slashing the windows, the house is quiet. Ma's not on the chesterfield or in her bedroom, drunk or sober. I rush from room to room, knowing Ma's not here, not yet ready to believe the cats are missing.

I search under the beds, behind the couch, in the closets, in the bathtub and the back room—and the whole time I'm aware of the stink of Javex, especially in the bathroom. The cats are nowhere in the house.

Trying to think, I stand still in the hall. The house is clean. Spotless. Ma must have taken herself to town as a reward for all her hard work. She's not supposed to clean, it being one of the jobs Da pays me to do.

I hurry to the back room, but the last bottle of Captain Morgan is still there in the crate, untouched. So Ma wasn't drinking when she left the house; she didn't let the cats out by mistake.

Somehow the Shrikes must have let them out. Even though the front door was locked.

My heartbeat goes manic. Who else could it have been but the Shrikes? In the storm, no one would have noticed them.

Or maybe it was just Tate.

The cats. I gotta find them.

I phone Travis to tell him Tansy and Rogue are missing. He says, "I'll search around here and work my way up the hill to your place. Don't worry, Prinny, we'll find them."

I pull on my oilskins and rubber boots. Outdoors, the rain slaps me in the face, while the wind makes me stagger. First off, I check around the house, screaming the cats' names. Then I let the wind push me over to the shed. "Tansy! Rogue!"

No sign of them. Holding to the side of the shed, I round the back corner out of the wind and take a deep breath, calling again. A ginger head pokes from under the shed, where the shingles don't meet the granite.

With a sob of relief, I bend down and pick Tansy up, kissing her wet fur, feeling her rub against my wet face. Gently I tuck her inside my jacket and brace myself to walk out into the wind again. But this time my legs feel strong. No nor'easter can get the better of me.

I'll go back once Tansy's dried off. I bet Rogue's still under the shed. For all the mischief he gets into, he can be real timid. I'll take cat treats with me— should've done that the first time.

In the house I take a towel from the bathroom,

wipe Tansy off, then put her down by her food bowl. She meows, shivering, rubbing herself against my legs, and I don't know if she's still cold or if she's remembering what a big scary place lies outside that door. After turning up the heat, I settle her on the rocker under an old mohair blanket.

"I have to find Rogue," I tell her, dropping more kisses between her ears. "I won't be long—you'll be fine."

Quickly I dial Travis's number, telling Rayleen Tansy's found and I'm going outside to rescue Rogue. Armed with a flashlight, I hurry straight to the back of the shed, crouch down, and toss some cat treats into the gap under the shed.

"Okay, Rogue. Time for your supper."

Nothing happens. Even though I strain my ears, I can't hear him crunching on the treats or meow-ing. Lying flat, I beam the flashlight under the shed. Rocks, a few slabs of wood, a couple of tattered plastic bags. That's it.

Slowly I stand up, fear tightening my throat. I was so sure he'd be under there, that he'd been keeping Tansy company. So where is he?

If I was Rogue, where would I go?

Da's never been one for painting the house—only time he picks up a brush is for *Wilma Marie*—but he did build it snug to the ground so critters couldn't get underneath. I circle the house again anyway, shouting Rogue's name, then I go to the neighbors on either side and check they didn't take him in.

He wouldn't be so stupid to run for the barrens, would he? Or toward the ocean on the other side of the road?

If Tate chased him, who knows where he went?

Head down, I cross the road, yelling Rogue's name. No shelter here from wind or rain, spray salty on my lips. I know Rogue's a couple of clues short of a load, but he's an animal and they're smarter than us when it comes to the outdoors.

He didn't fall in the sea and drown. No way.

Next I go to the little thickets of trees behind our house. I scream his name, then crouch again, searching low where the wind can't reach a lost and frightened cat. Gradually, taking my time and trying to keep my head, I quarter the area, using the flashlight because it's nearing dusk, the sky a mass of ragged purple gray clouds.

I'm out of sight of the house by now. All the different greens are being swallowed by the gloom, tamarack bowing and scraping, shadows looming among the boulders. Rocks ambush me, making me stumble and trip.

The barrens have always been the place I run to when the roller coaster's out of control. A friendly place, where I don't feel empty, where I'm more at home than in the house. But tonight, it's become the enemy. No one could find a cat out here in a nor'easter, a cat that's never once been outside the door. It's hopeless. Plain hopeless. The barrens stretch for miles, all the way to the Blue Hills.

"Prinny! Prinny, where are you?"

I wave the flashlight. "Over here!"

While Travis is a marvel on ice, he's a dud when it comes to keeping his footing on the barrens. But he reaches me in record time.

"You haven't found Rogue?" he gasps. "Me either. Listen, it's late, we'd better head home."

"I'm not going home until I find Rogue."

"You can't stay out here in the dark!"

I plant my feet. "Watch me."

"I'll tell your parents where you are—they'll be worried sick."

"Some chance." But Travis has gone and the words tear away on the wind.

I struggle to the next little copse of trees. Twigs snap and peat sucks at my boots as I lift the boughs to look for tracks in the patches of wet snow. Then I sweep my flashlight from one end to the other of a tumble of rocks, and follow them up the hill.

Because I've lost all sense of time, it's a shock when I hear Da's voice override the wind. I turn around and shout back. His flashlight wavers as he picks his way through the boulders; he's still in his oilskins and high waders, stubble on his chin. I want to hug him, just throw myself at him and lean on him.

He yells, "Travis arrived just when I got home, so I came right out here. Should've told Wilma where I was off to. Find anything?" I shake my head. "Fifteen minutes until full dark—how about you take the east side of the pond and I'll head west?"

With new energy I zigzag in the direction of the pond, hollering for Rogue until I'm hoarse, peering into every nook and cranny where a cat might tuck himself to keep dry. But when we meet back at the boulders in twenty minutes, neither of us has a gray cat under our oilskins.

"We better go home, Prinny," Da says.

"I don't want to!"

"You'll find him tomorrow. In daylight. Wind's supposed to drop by dawn."

Rogue might die of cold. A lynx could get him. Or the fox. With pups to feed, how could you blame the fox for nabbing a well-fed cat?

I'm crying, although I don't think Da can tell because of the rain running down my cheeks. All of a sudden, I'm so tired I could drown facedown in a puddle. Da's right. We can't search all night. We trudge back to the house, him leading the way, acting as a windbreak. In the porch we take off our gear.

"Thanks for helping me look, Da," I say, my voice wobbling.

Flustered, he says, "Let's go eat."

In the kitchen, Ma's standing by the stove holding a silver serving spoon like she's ready to rap us both on the head with it.

"Where've you been? Supper's dried up like codfish on a clothesline. You're gonna be this late, you could at least let me know. Ida's right, Prinny, you got no manners."

"The cats escaped and I went looking for them. Found Tansy, but Rogue...Rogue's still lost."

Ma's eyes shoot to the rocking chair, where Tansy's asleep in the mohair blanket. "Lost?"

"It's not your fault—the front door was locked when I came home."

Ma goes white. "Mother of God," she whispers.

Twenty

in·'cen·di·ar·y

Da says, "What's the matter, Wilma?"

Ma doesn't even look at him. She's staring at me, staring right through me. "I spilled some Javex this morning when I was cleaning the bathroom. House stank so bad and it wasn't raining then, so I opened both doors. Front and porch. To air the place out. Oh, Prinny…"

"*Both* doors were open?"

"For the better part of an hour. When I started cleaning, the cats were in your room—you know how they hate the vacuum cleaner. After that, I never even thought about them."

The Shrikes didn't let the cats out.

I'm icy cold inside, but white flames are shooting through my skull. I repeat, like I'm trying to memorize it, "You didn't think about the cats."

"I was desperate for a drink! That desperate I couldn't think at all. So I cleaned and cleaned, scrubbed floors, polished the furniture, vacuumed the rugs, anything to keep me away from the booze. And it worked. I didn't drink. Not a drop."

164

"You looking for a medal?" I say in a voice that doesn't sound like mine.

"Don't you talk to me that way! I didn't drink—don't you understand? So when I was done cleaning, I went to town, browsed Walmart and the mall. Didn't go near the liquor store."

"You let the cats out! Rogue's out there in the wind and rain—don't *you* understand?"

"I'm sorry, Prinny—I'm right sorry. But we'll find him in the morning. He won't have gone far."

"I don't ask you for much," I say in that same brittle voice. "But I did ask you to keep the cats in. You couldn't even do that for me. I love my cats, Ma. And why wouldn't I? Not much use loving you—here one day, gone the next, lying drunk outside Tony's Pizza for people to step—"

"Who told you that?"

"Kids at school. You think no one notices what you do? Why don't I have any friends? Because you'd turn up at school sloshed out of your mind. Grade two, me trying to climb on the school bus, you begging Mr. Murphy for a drive, cursing a blue streak. Grade three graduation, you staggering into the gymnasium, plunking yourself in Mr. Marsden's lap. All the kids laughing at me."

"Now, Prinny," Da says.

Ma's eyes are like pits. "But I—"

"Remedial reading—you ever wonder why I'm stuck with that? Coming home from school I never knew what I'd find. How was I supposed to do my homework? You never offered to help, never asked how things were going because you were too wrapped up in your own troubles. You never went to parent-teacher interviews either—you didn't care. All you care about is your booze, your frigging booze!"

"That's enough, Prinny!" Da thunders.

Now I'm turning those white flames on him. "Did *you* ever go see the teacher after Ma left? You ever ask me how I was doing? Long as your dinner's put in front of you sharp at five-thirty, you don't give a rat's ear what's going on in my life, and how come you never made me a headboard so I could sit up in bed and at least try to read? You could do it, you know you could. You just never bothered!"

Da looks stunned, like he hauled up a lobster trap and there was a stingray inside. "Headboard," he repeats stupidly.

"You didn't even notice the zipper was hanging off my j-jacket." Which is when the first sob bursts out of my mouth. I grab Tansy and run to my room, slamming the door so hard the shells rattle on the shelf. Tansy wriggles out of my arms and dives under the bed. I throw myself on top of it and wish I'd never been born.

When I wake up, the light's on and Tansy's curled up by my knees, fast asleep. The alarm clock says three minutes to midnight.

I'm hungry.

Rain's slapping against the window, wind rattling the screen. A whimper escapes me. Rogue's out there. Alone in the dark. And I'm complaining because I'm hungry?

My stomach rumbles. I'm not going near the kitchen if Ma or Da are still up. But I need to eat, then go to sleep again, so I can be up at daybreak to look for Rogue.

I lie still, blanking out the storm, listening. Then I slide off the bed, kiss Tansy, and very quietly open my door. The hall's dark, the door of Ma and Da's bedroom shut. No line of light under it.

One part of me is glad they're asleep. But the other part's mad as hops they could calmly go to bed after me screaming at them, pouring out stuff that's been brewing for years.

I know where all the creaking boards are. Besides, in a nor'easter you can make a fair racket without being heard. First thing I do is lean my weight against the front door to open it, and call Rogue. I'm praying hard as I can that a gray streak will whip past me into the house.

All that happens is my clothes get wet from the rain.

After turning on the light over the stove, I make a peanut butter and jam sandwich. The kitchen truly is clean. Cleaner than it's been in years.

Could you be so hard-pressed not to drink that nothing else matters? Not even your own daughter's cats?

I eat the sandwich in my room. Then I sneak down the hall to the back room. The bottle of Captain Morgan Rum is still lying in the crate on the closet floor.

I leave the bottle right where it is, and go back to bed.

At seven, when I wake up, the silence is what I notice first; Da said the wind would drop. Sun's glinting through my blinds. Maybe Rogue's come home, and he's sitting on the front step waiting to be let in.

I leap out of bed, startling Tansy, and hurry down the hall. Ma's sitting at the kitchen table with a mug of coffee. Bags under her eyes.

"He's not back," she says. "I just checked. Your Da's at the wharf. They'll be resetting their pots later."

I go outside anyway, in my pajamas and rubber boots. Raindrops sparkle in the sun. Rogue's nowhere to be seen.

When I go back in, the phone's ringing. Ma picks it up.

"Hello…No, he's still lost…Okay, here she is."

I clamp the phone to my ear. Travis says, "Me, Laice, and Hector are staying home from school to help you look for Rogue. We can come to your place in fifteen minutes, and we'll figure out a plan…Prinny, are you there?"

I find my voice. "Your dad, Hector's mum, and Laice's grandparents—they all agreed you guys could stay home?"

"I had to do some fast talking."

"I'll be ready."

I put down the phone. Ma says, "I'll make sandwiches."

Three friends. And they're all going to help me. By the time I've dressed and bolted down my cereal, they've arrived, standing in the porch like a little army. I give each of them a Ziploc bag of cat treats while Ma hands out sandwiches and juice packs.

"Thanks, Mrs. Murphy," Travis says. "Prinny, we came up with a plan. Laice will search around the backs of all the houses, Hector's taking his bike and checking both sides of the road to Fiddlers Cove, and I'll look around Abe's barn and along the Gulley Cove road—how's that?"

"I'll keep to the barrens then, where I left off last night," I say. "You guys are some nice to do this…we can cover a lot more ground with four of us."

"Let's meet back here in three hours," Travis says. "To check how we're doing."

"We'll find Rogue," Laice says, giving me her best smile. Hector grunts in agreement.

Ma speaks up. "I wants to help."

Travis looks flummoxed; we both know Ma's not one for the great outdoors. He says, "You could go along the street, Mrs. Murphy, and check out the gardens and the shoreline."

Ma nods and hauls on her jacket, then the five of us leave the house together and fan out to our different areas. The barrens are as beautiful as I've ever seen them—light dancing on the ponds, the spruce and juniper needles a fresh-rinsed green. It might have been a day for more of my short lines if Rogue wasn't lost.

I head south, calling for him and shaking the cat treats, keeping in mind that four other people are searching, not just me.

Takes quite a while to reach where Da and I quit last night; I'm well out of sight of the houses. Far in the distance, the Blue Hills live up to their name.

Back and forth I go, like a sailboat tacking into the wind. An hour passes, then another, until every nerve I own is stretched tight as Aunt Ida's hair. I'll have to leave soon to check in with the others.

Dogs run loose on the barrens. Last fall they killed

a cat at Gulley Cove; Travis was the one to find it.

I'd rather find Rogue's body than never know what happened to him.

I angle down a slope that's slippery with reindeer moss, concentrating on where to place my boots. When I glance up, my eyes catch a flash of rust red by a distant grove of trees. The fox, on the hunt. Today he feels like the enemy, same as the barrens did yesterday.

Not stopping to think, abandoning my plan of covering every inch of ground, I hurry toward those trees. One of my many faults—the gospel according to Aunt Ida—is that I have too much imagination. As I skid down the rock face and scramble knee-deep through the shrubs, I'm seeing the fox with Rogue clamped between his sharp, white teeth.

Rogue still alive. Bleeding. Meowing for help and me not quick enough to save him.

I'm almost at the trees when the fox streaks over the granite, uphill in the direction of his den. Nothing in his mouth. I stop dead, breathing hard, my knees trembling. First time I ever spooked him. Can't say I'm sorry.

"Rogue!" I yell and gulp down some juice.

Somewhere among the trees a cat meows.

Was *that* my imagination? Rooted to the ground, I call, "Rogue?"

Another meow, louder. I plunge into the trees, trying not to trip over rocks, and start shoving the boughs aside. "Rogue, where are you? You can come out now. You're safe."

The next meow is directly overhead. I look up, mouth agape. Rogue's twenty feet above me, anchored to a branch of the tallest spruce. He's swaying gently in the breeze, soaked to the skin, his eyes big as dinner plates.

"How did you get up there? The fox chased you, didn't he?"

So the fox *was* trying to turn my cat into breakfast. But at the same time, he helped me find Rogue. You have to wonder if life's ever simple.

Rogue's meow turns into a howl. A get-me-down-from-here-immediately howl. I try coaxing him down, rattling the treats and using my softest voice. He slithers to a lower branch. But there he stays, claws clinging to the bark. At least he chose the sturdiest spruce to climb, rather than a measly tamarack. I shuck off my jacket and choose my route.

None of the trees on the barrens grow big. So I don't have far to climb. Or—another way of looking at it—far to fall. Also, it's a youngish tree, so the branches don't crack when I put my weight on them. They bend, and so does the trunk, too much for my liking.

The boughs shower drops of water in my face.

My fingers stick to spruce gum on the bark. But step by step I get closer to Rogue, talking to him quietly, telling him what a brave cat he is and how he'll soon be home in his own bed.

When I'm nearly up to him, I grip the trunk between my knees, lean forward, and reach for him. Squealing like he never saw me before, he backs up. I make a grab for his shoulders. The tree dips. I squeal. My arms wrap themselves around the trunk like it's my best friend.

"Okay, Rogue, enough fooling around," I say, glaring at him. Prinny the Alpha Cat. This time when I reach for him, he settles himself on my shoulder meek as can be and digs his claws in. I scramble back down the tree.

Solid ground never felt so good. I shift Rogue from my shoulder, tuck my jacket around him, and tell him how much I love him. Then I feed him some treats, him purring loud as a snowmobile, and we start for home.

TWENTY-ONE
'con·se·quen·ces

Two and a half hours later, I'm back in school along with Travis, Laice, and Hector. Hector's mother drove us. Ma served us chicken noodle soup before we left. I didn't thank her. Not for that, or for searching the highway.

I'm waiting by the bus for Mr. Murphy after school, when along come the Shrikes.

Tate says, "So you found the cats. Too bad. We'll do it different, next time."

"You didn't do it. My ma did."

"Sure we did," Sigrid says.

"Yeah…just like you set Hud onto Travis."

Mel's scowling. "We didn't—"

"Shut up, Mel," Tate says.

"You didn't do it," I repeat stonily. "For starters, how'd you get there in the storm?"

"Sigrid's brother drove us right after school," Tate says. "We told him we had some books to deliver."

"The front door was locked," Sigrid says, "so we walked around the back and got in through a window.

174

One cat, the ginger one, was sleeping on the rocker in the kitchen. The gray cat was in your bedroom. Quite the bathmat on the floor."

"We shoved them out the same back window," Tate says.

I'm staring at her, sick to my stomach. Ma didn't let the cats out.

Last night I left the bottle of booze in clear sight in the crate. Wasn't I hoping Ma would latch onto it and drink herself pie-eyed, so Da would kick her out again?

Tate says, innocent as the day she was born, "I don't know why you're wearing a face long as Monday, Prinny. You found the cats…you should be smiling."

"Excuse me, girls," Mr. Murphy says, jingling his keys.

I'm the first one on the bus. I gotta hurry home. Apologize to Ma for all the bad things I said, and the good things I didn't say. Pray she didn't glom onto Captain Morgan.

Apologize? Am I out of my mind? With Ma out of the house, I'm off the roller coaster.

Off the roller coaster and bogged in guilt.

Laice sits with Travis, and somehow I manage to act halfway normal. Lucky thing Rayleen cancelled my cooking lesson; she had a dentist appointment. The bus stops at my place. I stand there gazing at the house. No truck, so Da's still at the wharf.

Apologize? Or scowl my way through the kitchen?

I kick at a clump of grass that's growing at the bottom of the driveway, digging at it with the toe of my boot until it's uprooted. Bending down, I toss it into the ditch. Then I start on the next clump.

"Prinny! Wait up!"

To my dismay, I see Laice running down the hill toward me. I start up the driveway, trying to look as though weeding the side of the road is something I do every day. She catches up with me before I reach the house. Puffing, she says, "I forgot we were going to read today because you're not with Rayleen. It'll be nice to see the cats again—I'm so glad they're safe."

As if I've become one of those robots, the kind that can't talk, I go inside, Laice on my heels. We take off our jackets in the porch. The house is quiet. Ma's gone to town, I think in huge relief. Shopping.

It's some easy to convince yourself of what you want to believe. When I lead the way into the living room, Ma's flat-out on the couch. An empty bottle of Captain Morgan is on the floor beside her, along with an empty glass, its rim smeared with lipstick. She sends a bleary smile in my direction. "Prinny darlin'…home already? I better start supper."

As she rolls over, she burps. She puts her hand to her mouth. "Oops."

I say, "Laice, get out of here." Laice makes a

choked sound. "Get out!"

Her socked feet slide across the floor. A few moments later, the front door opens and closes. I give Ma the same look I gave Rogue at the top of the tree.

"You're drunk. You can't get supper."

"Sure I can."

"You quit taking the pills from Dr. Keating?"

She looks at me slyly from under her lashes. "Must have forgot."

Any thoughts of apologizing have followed Laice out the door. "Three choices, Ma. One, take a pill and chase it with a long cold shower. Two, call a cab and leave now. Three, wait for Da to come home and kick you out."

For a split second, a scared little girl looks out her eyes. Then she's gone and it's Ma again. "I'll be okay," she says. "I only had a couple drinks."

"You drained the bottle." The bottle I left in the crate.

"Don't exagg…exaggerate," she says, pleased as punch she managed such a big word.

I open my mouth to speak, and I'll never know if my generous self or my mean-of-spirit self or even my guilty conscience would have won because someone comes in the front door. If it's Laice, I'll fix her clock.

Two boots hit the floor, bigger boots than Laice

will ever wear. Ma and me are staring at each other, both of us scared witless.

Then Da's standing in the doorway in his overalls and T-shirt, the one with burn holes from when he used to smoke. As he takes in the whole scene, I see how he'll look ten years from now.

"Wilma," he says, such hopelessness in his voice that I want to cry.

Ma tries to get to her feet. Her hand skids off the arm of the couch. Knock-kneed, she falls backward. "It was only two drinks, Tom."

"You know what I said—no drinking. You'll have to go back to Sebina and Ralph's."

"I forgot to take my pill!"

Rubbing the stubble on his chin, he gazes out the window like he'll find some answers there. "I'll go check, see if they'll take you back."

"One little mistake and you're sending me away?"

But Da's already left to make the phone call in the kitchen. Ma gets up, shoves past me, bangs her elbow on the door, and disappears into the kitchen. It's like always, neither one of them with the time of day for me.

I hear the rumble of Da's voice on the telephone. Ma says, like she's been shocked sober, "Don't send me away, Tom. *Please*."

"I can't help you. Not anymore."

Then he slouches down the hall to their bedroom, where I hear drawers opening and shutting. Ma stays put. Sounds like she's crying.

A few minutes later, Da goes back into the kitchen, carrying her suitcase. As though he's talking to a neighbor who happened to drop by, he says, "Your coat and boots are in the porch. I'll drive you over."

"Tom…"

Like I'm in a dream, I walk to the kitchen door. Da has his arm around Ma's shoulders, partly supporting her, partly pushing her into the porch. He closes the porch door. Next thing you know, the truck drives away.

I have the house to myself. The way I like it. I better check out the refrigerator because Da'll be hungry when he comes home.

As I peel potatoes and carrots and put them on to boil, I feel as if someone else is doing it, someone not even related to me. I open a bottle of caribou meat and make gravy from the juice. When the vegetables are near to tender, I drain them and throw everything together. Canned peas and bread with it—that'll have to do.

I never said good-bye to Ma. No big deal, compared to everything else that's lead-heavy on my conscience. *Oh, by the way, Da, the Shrikes let the cats out. Not Ma. And I left booze in a place where I knew she'd find it. So maybe you were a mite hasty dumping her on Aunt Sebina and Uncle Ralph.*

I like Uncle Ralph. He's got a face like a friendly moose. Aunt Sebina's nice, too. She's always happy to see me, and won't hear criticism of anyone. "There but for the grace of God," she says, and hands out another molasses cookie.

She'll always take Ma in. Says that's what sisters are for.

I set the table with clean place mats, trying to recover the feeling that I'm in charge in my own kitchen.

Da comes home looking like a beaten dog. He pushes his food around on his plate, then leaves the table, turns on the TV, and slumps in front of it.

Once I've cleaned up the dishes, I go to my room. The lemonade book falls open at the chapter that's about LaVaughn's dad. When I start there, I see two little words: *he died.* Even though I don't want to know how he died, I can't seem to stop reading.

LaVaughn's dad was shot by someone in a gang. By mistake.

I'm blinking back tears. LaVaughn has so much on her plate, what with the awful place she babysits, and her having no father because he was murdered. But she's doing her best.

Unlike some I could mention.

TWENTY-TWO

sep·a·'ra·tion

When Laice gets on the bus the next morning, she ignores me, sits down next to Travis, and talks up a storm. Same goes for the day after. At home, Da's scarcely talking to me, and from what I overheard when he was on the phone with Aunt Sebina, Ma's hitting the clubs.

On Friday, although Laice is still behaving as though my head's hatching nits, Travis has that look that means he's gearing up for action. At recess, I work on keeping my distance from the Shrikes—not that they're making any moves my way. Makes me right edgy, wondering how long before Tate jumps me. Then I see Travis and Laice off in a corner, arguing something fierce. What's that all about?

When Laice gets on the bus after school, she sits across the aisle from me. Looking past my left shoulder, she says, "I'm coming to your place."

"When?"

"Now."

"What for?"

"You'll find out."

I've been feeling off-color all day, and now this. "Maybe I don't want you at my place."

"Too bad."

She sits in a stony silence for the rest of the ride. Mr. Murphy lets us both off at the bottom of my driveway. I'm not inviting her in. Look what happened last time.

"What's up?" I say.

"Travis got on my case at recess. He says I owe you an apology."

"Well, you don't. So you can go home right now."

"You're not the only girl in Ratchet with problems!"

"Gee…did you spill something on your white carpet? Or is your fancy stereo on the fritz?"

Laice takes a step backward, her face frozen. But she can't freeze her eyes, such pain swimming in them that I gabble, "I'm sorry, I'm sorry. Sometimes the devil rides my tongue."

"You seem to think you're unique!"

"No one else around here has a drunk for a mother!"

"I like your mother when she's sober," Laice says. "But when she's not, there's no need for you to act as if I'm dispensable."

"Dispensable?" At least I knew what *unique* meant.

"Something you throw out when you're done

with it. Like a Kleenex you've blown your nose on."

"Is *that* how you feel?"

"You couldn't wait to push me out the door the other day."

"I never had a girlfriend, Laice. I blew it, I know I did—I was upset about finding Ma drunk. No, that's not it. Not all of it…I was shamed you saw Ma drunk."

The truth. For once. I wait for her to say we're finished.

She says, "You're not telling me anything I don't already know."

Feeling dumb, feeling desperate, I say, "I-I still want us to be friends."

"You'd better hold off on that one."

She's not making any sense. "Why don't we go inside?" I say. "No one's home. Ma's living in St. Fabien again and Da's at the wharf."

In the kitchen I take charge, making tea, putting ginger cookies on Ma's ceramic plate, jabbering about the cats. But finally there's nothing left to do but sit down. I reach for a cookie.

Laice is picking at a thread on her cuff. "I've been lying to you ever since I arrived. Lying to everyone. Including Travis."

My hand stops in midair. "What do you have to lie about?"

"Aren't you mad at me? Lies are serious."

When it comes to Ma and me, my life is one big lie. "No."

"Really?"

Laice Hadden from Halifax is worrying that Prinny Murphy from Ratchet will cut her off—dispense with her—because of a few lies? "Cross my heart."

"My mum and dad aren't on a cruise." Her voice quivers. "They're separating."

She's unraveled the thread from her sweater. I do the only thing I can think of, which is to hold her fingers still. "I'm sorry, Laice. Real sorry."

A tear drips on the back of my hand. "They sent me here so I'd be out of the way. They sent my sister to my other—"

"Your *sister*?" I feel a sharp pang of envy.

"Lynette. She's ten. We fight a lot, but I really miss her." Another tear trickles off my hand. "She's with our Hadden grandparents, in Fredericton. I couldn't tell anyone about my parents, I just couldn't. So I lied. I pretended to you and Travis—and even to myself—that they were on a cruise, and when they came back, everything would be fine."

I blurt, "Which one will you live with?"

"Both of them want custody of me—of me and my sister. So they hired lawyers to fight it out. They'll be going to court sometime soon, and a judge will decide."

"A judge? Someone you don't even know?"

The tears are coming steady now. "Why can't they share me? It's not like I'm a house or a swimming pool—I'm their daughter!"

I have this nasty image of Laice with lobster twine around each wrist, her father winching her east and her mother west. I wish I had something wise to say, something that would really help, but my mind's gone blank. Only thing I can do is keep my hand on hers and wish with all my heart that her parents would smarten up.

Finally I say, "They wouldn't split you up, would they? You and your sister?"

"I don't know…I don't know anything anymore. All they do is fight. Awful fights. Screeching and yelling." Her voice shakes. "They hate each other. So if my sister goes with Mum and I go with Dad, I may never see Lynette again."

"Do your grandparents know the truth?"

"They've known since the beginning." Wiping her eyes, she says, "Sometimes I wish I could stay right here, with Gran and Gramps."

"I'd like that."

"It's not going to happen." She bites her lip. "Travis thought I was ignoring you because your mother started drinking again. I knew you were ashamed of her that day—the same way I'm ashamed of my parents.

So when he kept bugging me, I told him about the separation. He suggested I tell you the truth." She grimaces. "It wasn't just a suggestion. It was an order."

"Mr. Fix-It."

Laice makes a sound between a giggle and a hiccup. "You've got his number."

"Thanks for telling me, Laice." I'm pitifully close to tears myself.

"You'll keep it a secret? I don't want the kids at school knowing."

"I will," I say, solemn as if I'm taking a vow in church.

"It makes you lonesome when you have a big secret you can't share."

Doesn't seem the time to tell her about me and the booze.

TWENTY-THREE
ˈbod·y ˈlan·guage

I don't feel too grand after Laice leaves. My back aches, dull and low-down; I must have been sitting crooked in the chair. Being a proper girlfriend is no bed of roses. Bed of nettles, more like. Although Laice looked so perfect the first time we met, I'm beginning to think *perfect* only exists in easy readers. She's been stuck-up and mean, and she's been lying to Travis and me. But she helped with Rogue, she wants to be my friend, and she doesn't give a dead sculpin that my ma's a drunk.

When I look in the refrigerator to see what I'll make for supper, my stomach goes queasy. Maybe I'm coming down with the flu. I turn on the radio good and loud to cheer me up, last of the Top Forty, then a call-in show. But as I'm standing at the sink peeling the potatoes, I realize something else is going on. Something I've been wondering about for months. I hurry to the bathroom.

The curse, Ma calls it. Becoming a Woman, according to the health nurse at school. Either way, I got no pads.

I hobble to Ma's dresser and start going through

it, drawer by drawer. In the very bottom drawer I find some light-day pads. Better than nothing, so I pick up the box.

Underneath is a plain brown envelope. BIRTH CERTIFICATES, it says. My brow squinches like Da's. Ma and Da only had the one kid. Me.

I reach for the envelope. Behind me, Da says, "What are you doing in here, Prinny?"

"Da! I didn't hear you come in."

"Radio's loud enough to deafen the dead."

The box is still in my hand. Heat rises up my neck clear to my forehead. "I need to go to Baldwin's Store. Will you drive me?" What if I leak on the way, like Fay Murphy in gym class?

He looks from the box to my red cheeks and back at the box. "This your first time?" he says. I nod. He says, "I'll go to the store."

"You don't mind buying female stuff?"

"Rather be caught in a squall north of Knuckle-bones," he says, dead-serious. "But I've done it for your ma. Reckon I can do it for you."

I drop the box on top of the envelope and nudge the drawer shut with my toe. "I can pay."

"No need for that. Don't you bother cooking— beans and wieners will do us just fine."

"I already peeled the potatoes."

"Then I'll buy some sausages and fry them up."

My voice sounds like Laice's, quivery. "Thanks, Da."

"You go sit down," he says. "Tomorrow you better stay off the boat. Once I'm home, if you're up to it, we'll do groceries."

Him being so nice to me, so kind, makes my plan all the worse. Tomorrow, while he's on the water, I'm going to open that envelope.

First thing I pull out of the envelope is Ma and Da's marriage certificate. Wilma Marie Quinn, spinster, and Thomas Eavan Murphy, bachelor, both of this parish. The date leaps out at me. It doesn't take two seconds to calculate they were married six months before I was born.

I sit down on the edge of their bed. My hands are cold, and I have to bend over suddenly from a cramp. It was my fault they got married. Is that why Ma and me always been at odds? Is that why she drinks?

I should put the envelope back and forget I ever opened it.

The next two sheets are birth certificates. The date on both of them is the date of my birthday in December.

Two girls.

Prinny Bethiah and Janie Elizabeth. Both born in St. Fabien Hospital. Me first, Janie second, ten minutes apart.

Twins. I had a twin sister.

I know what I'm going to see before I look at the last piece of paper. A death certificate. Janie Elizabeth, my sister Janie, was stillborn.

Too stunned to cry, I grip the papers as though I'm waiting for Janie Elizabeth to speak to me. The house creaks in the wind. Tansy comes trotting in, jumps up on the bed, and starts washing her face. But I'm somewhere else. The gap, that emptiness I've felt for as long as I can remember, there was a reason for it. For nine months, Janie and I lived inside Ma, side by side, learning to kick and suck our thumbs, listening to Ma's heartbeat, *thumpety-thump, thumpety-thump*. Both of us as close as sisters can be.

But something went wrong and she died.

Tears plop on the death certificate. Hurriedly I wipe it with a tissue and put the papers back in the envelope. Then I shove the envelope in the drawer under the box of light-days. All these years I could have had a sister. The sister I've always longed for without knowing why.

It's only eight o'clock in the morning. I pick up Tansy, go to my room, and climb back in bed, pulling the covers over my head. My feet are cold, but nowhere near as cold as my heart. Secrets. Too many secrets.

Laice was right. They make you lonesome.

By four-thirty Da and me have the groceries loaded in the truck, we've been to the dollar store, and we're heading home along Main Street. Every step of the way, I feel the presence of my sister Janie, so real it's a wonder Da doesn't notice her.

The east end of Main Street goes past the Schooner Tavern, its parking lot full of cars and trucks. Ma and the guy with the skimpy black beard are standing on the steps. They're having an argument, Ma yelling at him, him yelling right back. He grabs her by the elbows and shakes her. He's a big guy, near as big as Da. Her head flops like she's a rag doll; she'd have fallen if he wasn't still holding her, holding her so high that her toes barely touch the step.

Da jams the brakes on and he's out the door faster than I knew he could move. He barrels across the street, clumsy-like, but covering the ground. I slide out of the truck and run after him. I'm not letting Da get beat up by some guy with a stupid little beard.

Da stops four feet away from the guy. He says, real quiet, "I know you—Zack Rollins from St. Christopher. Put Wilma down."

"Yeah? Why should I?"

"She's my wife."

"Tom," Ma says, tugging to free her sleeve, "what are you doing here?" Sounds like she's sober.

Zack Rollins says, "Make me."

In a blur of movement Da chops at Zack's wrist. Zack gives a howl of pain and drops Ma. Da puts an arm around her so she doesn't fall. Not taking his eyes off the guy, he says, "Stay away from her, you hear?"

Zack mutters, "She's half-cut most of the time anyways," and stumbles into the tavern, clutching his wrist.

Da looks square at Ma, and it's only now that he raises his voice. "Enough of this foolishness! You're coming home, Wilma—where I'll make damn sure you take them pills even if I have to sit on you. One a day. Until the day you drop dead, needs be."

Five seconds dead silence. I stand like a stick. Ma ducks free of his arm. "Home?" she says. "That's a change of tune—you're the one who kicked me out. Twice."

"Your daughter started her monthlies yesterday and you—her mother—nowheres to be found. Your husband needs you—day and night. Home, that's where you're going. Home. For good."

"For good?" Ma says. "Without the booze, there's no good in me."

"Crap," Da says.

Ma jerks at her jacket, straightening it with an angry snap. "You don't need me! You never have— I'm just your wife. The sea's your mistress, Tom. Has been as long as I can remember."

"I never made no secret the sea's in my blood."

"Your boat gets a fresh coat of paint every spring, and the smallest thing goes wrong with her, you—"

"Out there in the reefs, your life depends on your boat."

"When did you last paint the house, you tell me that! Big flakes peeling off the porch, cracked linoleum in the kitchen, no cupboards in the bathroom. Your daughter with no headboard for her bed. I know your priorities, Tom Murphy, and they ain't me and they ain't our house."

"You got it wrong," Da says; he's back to quiet. "You're the dock I leaves from, Wilma, and the dock I comes home to. Always have been, ever since we met. Always will be."

A couple of gulls swoop down, checking the parking lot for scraps, their screams harsh and wild. Ma gives herself a little shake. Not sounding quite so sure of herself, she says, "Prove it. Do some work around the house, instead of helping Dave Baldwin or gabbing with your buddies at the wharf. I'm a Quinn from Fiddlers Cove—you know what they calls us. Scum buckets, every last one of us. I wants to live in a house that looks decent. Cared for."

"I never knew the house was a bother to you."

"Antique green, with dark green trim and window boxes so we can plant geraniums and marigolds. I can scrape shingles and slap on a coat of paint, sure. But I needs your help."

"Okay."

"You never—what do you mean, *okay*?"

"I'll paint the house. But you'll have to go up the ladder, Wilma. You know I'm scared to death of heights."

"You scared of heights. Me scared of the water. We're a fine pair," Ma mutters. But she's smiling. She says, "Did you mean all that stuff about docks?"

Da drops his hands on her shoulders. "Every word."

"A woman likes to hear that kind of thing every so often, Tom." Her face goes soft. "Keep that in mind, why don't you?"

Once again, I'm left out of the loop. Three men from Fiddlers Cove walk past us and go inside the tavern. I turn around to walk back to the truck, which is still sitting at an angle on Main Street, cars swinging around it.

Ma says, "Wait, Prinny, we'll cross the street together."

Once we're in the truck, me in the cab instead of up front with Da, she twists in her seat. "I'm right sorry you had to start your monthlies and me not home."

I should confess now. This minute. But they both look so happy, Da humming as he puts the key in the ignition, Ma smiling at me. If I spill my guts just so I'll feel better, I'll wreck something rare and precious.

So I don't say, "Ma, Tate Cody let the cats out," or, "Da, I left a bottle in plain sight in the back room for Ma to find." I don't say, "I didn't need you when I got the curse, Ma, because Da went to Baldwin's for me." I certainly don't say, "How come you never told me I had a twin sister?"

Instead I say, "I had cramps yesterday. You ever get them?"

"I can give you something for them," she says, woman to woman. "I'm glad you were home, not at school."

"Me, too!"

She laughs a little, and, amazingly, so do I.

Da says, "Let's go to Pizza Delight for supper. No one wants to cook tonight."

I grin at him in the rearview mirror. "Cold sausages in the fridge."

"We'll eat 'em tomorrow. Today's special."

As the three of us dig into a large pizza with the works, it does feel special. Ma drinks ginger ale and flirts with Da, who sits as close to her as he can and wolfs down his pizza. His smile is big enough to surround her and me. I chew pepperoni, green peppers, and onions; the flavors mingle on my tongue. Happiness is tricky stuff.

There's a butterfly called a spring azure, first one to appear on the barrens when the weather starts to warm; its wings look like it clipped tiny triangles from the sky and flew away with them. Perhaps happiness is like that butterfly, chancy as a blue sky.

When we're back in the truck, driving home through the dark, Ma says, "I never once seen you hit anyone, Tom. Not until today."

"No one roughs up my wife."

"I wish I'd had you around when I was a little girl," Ma says, such pain in her voice that the special feeling wavers in the air, flops to the floor.

"Your father wouldn't have laid a finger on you, Wilma, if I'd been around."

I shiver. Last time I saw Hud on the bus, he had an ugly yellow bruise on the back of his hand, which was crisscrossed with scabs. At least Ma has Da to protect her. But who's Hud got to protect him from Uncle Doyle? A three-year-old called Fleur?

Couple of Sundays ago Father Gogan preached on a verse in the Bible where the fathers had eaten some sour grapes. The upshot? Their children's teeth were set on edge. For all he never goes to church, Hud knows everything there is to know about that verse, and so does Ma. She didn't want to have children because she didn't want the sour grapes passed on. But she got pregnant anyway. Pregnant with twins.

I'd better add snooping in Ma's drawer to my list of sins. I'll be saying Hail Marys for the rest of my days.

I'm not going to confess to her or Da. The Shrikes and a bottle of Captain Morgan are minor league compared to Janie Elizabeth. Besides, Ma already knows about the rum; she's the one who drank it. She knows I left it in the back room on purpose. As if I hate her.

Believing your only daughter hates you would be enough to make anyone drink.

TWENTY-FOUR

tee′ter-tot′ter

On Sunday after church, Laice and me read the whole chapter about LaVaughn's dead father, then we move on to the next chapter. I'm desperate to tell her about my twin sister. But I can't force the words past my tongue. Worse, the emptiness is back.

Laice doesn't notice anything's wrong. In the cafeteria at noon on Monday, we practice the first few pages of the book. Last period, when Mrs. Dooks joins me at the back of the room for remedial reading, I say, "Can I read from my own book today, Mrs. Dooks?"

"I suppose so," she says and asks to see the book. "That's too advanced for you."

"The short lines help," I say, my fingers cold as I take the book back and open it. "I'll begin at the beginning."

At first I mess up some of the words even though I know them so well. Two of the kids snicker. But LaVaughn's voice, so clear in my head, calms me down. The words fall into place, and first thing you know I'm finishing the third chapter in part one.

As I pause for breath, Mrs. Dooks says, "Did you memorize it?"

"No! I've been practicing."

She takes the book from me and opens it to part three; Laice and me are still in part one. "Can you read that?"

The letters jitter around. My brain goes clumsy. But the first seven words are short ones. Then I come to *ain't* and I know that word, and *social studies*, and I keep going, and it's about LaVaughn not being allowed to say *ain't* by her mom; and I bowl along pretty good, wanting to know how it turns out, her mom being a force to reckon with.

Mrs. Dooks interrupts. "Excellent," she says, which is a word I can't ever recall her saying to me before. "You managed this on your own?"

"I had help. Dr. Keating. Travis and Laice." I take a risk. "LaVaughn helped most of all."

"She's a true hero," Mrs. Dooks says.

"Yeah! That's what she is! So you know about this book?"

"I read it a long time ago." Mrs. Dooks looks at her watch. "The bell will be ringing any minute. We'll read from it again next week. Keep up the good work, Prinny."

"Oh, I will, don't you worry." I'm prancing on air, I'm that excited. Laice is smiling as I go back to my seat, and Travis gives me a high-five.

Janie would be happy for me, too. I know she would.

Right after supper, Ma swallows her pill—that being a time of day Da's always around. Then he takes out his wallet and passes me two ten-dollar bills. "Two weeks' wages," he says, winking at me.

"Thanks, Da." I shove them in the pocket of my jeans.

Later, back in my room, I rummage under my socks for the envelope where I keep the money. Soon as I lift it, I know something's wrong. The envelope's empty. I shake it, turn it upside down as though ten-dollar bills are going to rain from it, then search among my socks until everything in the drawer is topsy-turvy, socks and underwear and the training bra I've never taken out of the package. No money. Not one red cent.

Da's been paying me ten dollars a week regular, and I only gave Tate eighty. I should have over ninety dollars.

Somebody took it. Ma. How else could she afford the clubs and taverns?

I'm so angry I'm around the end of the bed and out in the hall before I know it. Then I put on the brakes, slippers skidding on the pine boards. Sure, Prinny, go ahead. Confront Ma about your money.

And the follow-up? A full and complete confession of all *your* sins?

Luckily Da and Ma are watching TV in the living room. I creep back to my room and sit on the bed, smoothing the quilt.

The gray cat was in your bedroom. Quite the bathmat on the floor…

Tate and Sigrid were in my room, looking for Rogue. Either one of them could have gone through my drawers and found the envelope. I'd wager every cent I own—all twenty dollars of it—on Tate.

If she did steal the money, she knows I was lying when I said I was flat broke. I stand up quick and close my blinds.

Ma or the Shrikes: who *did* take the money? I can't ask Ma, even if I ask real gentle. It might send her off the deep end, my conscience sinking alongside her. But—I realize with a little shock of surprise—keeping silent isn't just about my conscience. It's about me being kinder to Ma. Generous of spirit. The good twin in me rising up stronger than the bad twin.

Why is it so much harder to be good than bad? Does that explain all the *shalt nots*? Mind you, Jesus was hot on people loving their neighbors, a *thou shalt* which sounds okay until you add the last bit, which is about loving yourself. They don't teach you how to do that in school. Or anywhere else that I know of.

After I hide the two ten-dollar bills in the pocket of an old pair of jeans I never wear anymore, I do my homework. Then I spend half an hour on phonics and go over the last few chapters we read in my lemon-ade book. The next chapter's short. Because of self-respect, which LaVaughn has, I work on those two pages by myself.

When the bell rings to end recess, the early morning fog is long gone and it's started to rain. Laice runs ahead of me to get in line. I walk slower. I love the splash of raindrops cool on my face. The air smells different when it rains...the sea comes closer, even the dirt rises up to meet you...

Two hands shove me hard in the chest. My back hits the brick wall.

Mel's teeth are bared in a big smile. Tate's on one side of her, Sigrid on the other. Tate says, razor-sharp, "Twenty-five bucks. Tomorrow. Don't do the innocent, I-got-no-cash routine because we're not buying it."

"The money you stole out of my drawer was from Da paying me for housework when Ma wasn't home. But she's back now, and she's staying. So I don't have any money and that's the God's truth."

I shouldn't dress up a lie using God's holy name. Still, I'm in so deep, one more sin scarcely signifies.

"Twenty-five bucks or you're dead meat," Tate says. Mel kicks me in the shin, the toe of her boot bruising me to the bone.

The three of them head for the door. Rubbing my leg, I limp after them. I *am* in trouble. Because I'm not handing over my last twenty dollars to that crew. I'm not.

Rayleen teaches me how to make bakeapple cheese-cake at Travis's place after school. By the time I get home, the fog's thick around the house. Da's already been to the hardware store and bought wood for my headboard, smooth birch planks that still smell of the forest.

"Once I've finished this," he says, "I'll pick up a piece of Cushionfloor for the kitchen and see if I can get a deal on some oak for kitchen cabinets."

Normally, I'd be real happy he's making me a headboard, especially out of real wood, not pressed plywood. "Thanks, Da," I say, knowing if I hug him I might not be able to let go. "Maybe I'll use a clear stain on it so the grain will show."

"Tom, I'll go with you when you pick out the flooring," Ma says. "Cushionfloor's on sale next week."

After supper, Da goes out to the shed to start on the headboard, so Ma and me do the dishes together, her washing, me drying.

Out of the blue, she says, "The day I let the cats out—I'm glad now you ripped into me. I been thinking about it, about what kind of mother I been to you since I started on the rum. In a weird way, you finally telling me the truth about how you felt—it honored me." She slops the suds over a plate, her head bent. "Don't know if that makes any sense."

"You're doing good, Ma," I whisper. Shouldn't I tell her the Shrikes pushed the cats out the window? It'd make her feel better about herself. But if I do, it'll lead smack-dab to the bottles of rum I left in the back room closet. How mean was that. So mean my spirit cringes.

Ma rinses the plate, then stacks it in the rack. "I'm trying to make things right. Uphill work, I can tell you. So I'm joining AA." She grabs another plate and starts scrubbing it hard enough to take the pattern off. "I been drinking a long time. I'm scared I'll start again and wreck everything."

I'm scared, too. But should I say so? "We're rooting for you, Da and me."

I am. I really am.

She drops the cloth, rubs her hands down her jeans, leaving two trails of bubbles, and hugs me, a hug that's like a bird folding its wings around me. Then her hands dive back into the sink. "Let's go to the store on the weekend to pick out paint colors for the house," she says.

"Okay."

The sky-blue butterfly from Pizza Delight flits toward me, takes one look at all the secrets I'm hoarding, and backs off fast. But when the sun breaks through the fog early the next morning, I find myself hoping the butterfly's outside my window, spreading its wings to warm itself. I have to do something. I can't go on feeling so unhappy, day after day. But I'm like Ma; I need help. Is there a Deceitful Daughters Anonymous?

The answer's right in front of me. Da's got big shoulders. I'll tell him about leaving the bottles in the closet. Assuming he doesn't give me the chop— like he did Zack Rollins—I could explain about Janie Elizabeth at the same time.

I'll get off the bus in Fiddlers Cove after school, catch him at the wharf before he heads home.

Right now, I could dance with a dozen butterflies. I forget all about Tate's twenty-five dollars until she climbs on the bus, Sigrid right behind her. Before I know it, I'm on my feet. "Tate," I say, loud enough that even the kids at the back go quiet, "I don't care if you set Mel on me or not—I'm done giving you money. So lay off."

Omigosh. What have I done? Tate looks like she could skin me alive. Sigrid looks scared. One of the Fiddlers Cove girls laughs from pure nerves.

Mr. Murphy says, "Tate, you been putting the squeeze on kids again? Prinny's right—lay off, or you'll land in trouble."

I sit down. Travis waves his arms in the air like I just scored a goal. Laice grips my sleeve. "Good for you," she says, none too quiet herself.

"Shush," I mutter. "Me in Tate's black books is more than enough."

As the bus gears up, the Herbey girls start talking again. If I get off in Fiddlers Cove this afternoon, Tate and Sigrid will be onto me so fast I won't get anywhere near the wharf. Only way I can talk to Da today is if I sneak out to the shed this evening while he's making my headboard.

But as soon as the dishes are done, Ma says, "Think I'll keep Tom company in the shed, Prinny. You okay with that?"

"Sure, Ma. I have homework to do."

Serves me right that I can't get near Da. Tomorrow night is Ma's first AA meeting; he'll probably come home from the wharf early so he can drive her. Still, on Saturday him and me will be out on the boat, no Ma with us then. I can hang on until Saturday.

Thursday goes by. The fog's offshore, so the boats will have gone out. Hector, Laice, Cole, Buck, and Stevie stick around at recess and lunch, same as they did the day before. For protection, Travis says.

I have more friends than I know what to do with.

Friday the fog hangs around, so thick you can't see across the road. Ma tells me at breakfast—which she made for me, French toast and bacon—that Da and some of his buddies will be at the wharf all day, mending pots that were damaged in the nor'easter. Lobstermen don't mess with fog around here, too many reefs.

Tate and Sigrid aren't in school, nor is Mel; they sometimes give themselves a three-day weekend. Although I could wait until tomorrow to talk to Da, I'd rather do it today so he'll have time to ponder. Then, if the fog lifts, we can talk some more on the boat on the weekend. Da doesn't like being rushed, whether he's sanding a headboard or puzzling how to handle his daughter.

I wait until the first stop in Fiddlers Cove before I say to Laice and Travis, "I want to catch Da at the wharf. See you guys later."

Travis sits up straight. "I'm coming with you. Me and Laice."

"You can't—I need to see Da on my own."

"What about Tate and Sigrid?"

"They're at the mall, sure. And Da will drive me home."

"I'm going to phone your place after supper, make sure you're back."

Mr. Murphy says, "You getting off, Prinny?"

"Yeah. See you later, Laice."

She's looking at me, narrow-eyed. I say, "I promise I'll tell you all about it Saturday afternoon," because by then my conscience should be on the up and up. I climb down the steps of the bus with Cole and Buck. The bus drives away, the guys run up Buck's driveway and disappear inside his house, and I'm left alone in the fog.

TWENTY-FIVE

'sis·ter·hood

There's not another soul in sight. I wish I'd asked Buck and Cole to stick around until I found Da.

Hud's place is at the other end of Fiddlers Cove. For a moment I have the crazy idea of hiking there and asking him to walk to the wharf with me. But Hud's got enough troubles without adding mine.

I set off down the road, heading west. In a few minutes I pass Cole's place, which is the last house in the cove. The road to the wharf veers down the hill, the pavement broken up from the frost last winter. Little drops of moisture cling to my jacket like gray fur, and I wonder how the foxes are doing. The fog-horn moans like a seal.

It'd be some easy to get lost in a mist thick as this. Then the first building looms ahead with its red-and-white Government of Canada sign. No trucks though, so I guess some of the men must have gone home. Creepy being down here by myself, even though I've been here with Da more times than I can count.

With a lift of relief, I hear muffled voices.

I hurry toward them. Da usually parks near the end of the wharf because it saves him hoofing it; he's never been a fan of using his legs to go from here to there.

Someone steps out of the fog. In sheer terror I see it's Mel. She gapes at me, holding a cigarette in front of her mouth in her big fingers. Then she says loudly, "Lookit who's here—Tate, we got company."

I hear the scrape of footsteps and whirl, my heart racing. Tate's smoking as well, Sigrid standing behind her. Tate smiles, a smile that fills me with dread. "We were about to have a few beers," she says. "But now we got something better to do."

Does that mean the wharf's deserted? That Da's already left?

They're blocking the way I came, the way to houses and people and safety. Quick as a flash I lunge sideways and make a mad dash for the far end of the wharf. *Be there, Da*, I pray. *Please, please be there*.

Waves suck at the pilings. Mel's pounding after me, but it's Tate I'm afraid of, her quicker footsteps, her vicious temper.

Da's truck is gone. I'm such a dummy—why didn't I let Travis come with me?

Tate yells, "No need to rush—Prinny ain't going nowheres." Then she laughs. "We got her where we want her. Oh, Prinny, you'll wish you never opened your mouth on that bus."

The foghorn nearly blasts my ear off. I drop my backpack near the creosoted boards. Then I'm over the top, fingers gripping cold metal as my feet find the second rung of the ladder. Hand over hand, rung after rung, quick as I can. Our little wooden dory's at its usual mooring, rocking gently on the tide. High tide, I notice with a distant part of my brain. Hands shaking, I loose the hawser, toss it in the bow, and jump in.

The dory lurches; I almost lose my balance. Tate gives a screech of rage and starts down the ladder. Mel fires a rock at me. But I've grabbed the oars, jamming one against the wharf and pushing off with all my strength. The rock bangs on the gunwale and bounces into the sea.

No time for oarlocks. I sit down hard on the thwart, thrust both oars into the water, and pull as I've never pulled before, stronger on the right one to bring the bow away from the wharf. As Tate grasps a rung with one hand, I swear her fingers brush the end of the oar. I dig it into the water and haul on it. She lunges for the stern. For a horrible moment I think she's going to jump aboard.

My next stroke makes the dory surge ahead.

Mel throws a gaff at me like it's a spear. The metal hook scrapes my arm, the wooden handle banging against the oar. The dory falters.

The gaff splashes into the sea, floating to stern. Gritting my teeth against the pain, I row harder. Another stone grazes my cheek, and three more clatter into the bottom of the dory. But the wharf's disappearing, swallowed in the mist, and the Shrikes are swallowed with it.

Quickly I shove the oars into the oarlocks and settle into a rhythm of dip and pull, dip and pull, throwing my whole weight into each stroke. They might come after me in Pete Herbey's dory, which is moored behind *Wilma Marie*; I'm pretty sure Sigrid knows her way around boats. My breath heaves in my chest. My cheek stings. Is this how the fox feels when dogs bay on the barrens?

The wharf's vanished. I'm surrounded by gray, the water a darker gray that gurgles at the bow, slurps from the stern. I brace my heels against a rib, knowing that every stroke is putting distance between me and Tate. But eventually I stop, oars shipped as I listen for any sound of pursuit. No dip of oars into the sea. No roar of an engine. Only the eerie wail of the foghorn...*the wharf's this way, come closer, come closer*.

The tide's just on the turn, carrying me with it, and for several minutes I drift. The wind freshens offshore. The Shrikes are probably still lying in wait for me, so I should stay out here a while longer.

I was some lucky to escape from them.

The foghorn moans again. I'm marooned in a small circle of ocean, the dory bobbing in its center. I'm alone, completely alone.

At the stern, out of the mist, the shadowy outline of a girl appears. She's like mist herself, like a deep pool of calm. Janie Elizabeth. My sister. My fingers tighten around the oars; the wood feels warm and smooth against my palms.

"If you'd lived," I say to her, "you'd have protected me from the Shrikes. And I'd have protected you. Always."

My head drops to my chest, grief an ache in my heart. I can't cry, it goes too deep for tears. All those years of emptiness. No friends. Kids mean to me at school. Ma off doing her thing with Captain Morgan. Da too wrapped up in Ma, his buddies, and his boat to realize he had a daughter who wanted to hug him and didn't dare.

I wish Janie hadn't died. Oh, how I wish she hadn't died. She won't ever breathe the cold salt of the sea, or smell crowberries on the barrens. She's missed out on Ma's smile and the way Da squinches his face when he's thinking.

She never knew me, her own sister.

A wave slops against the bow, splashing me. I gotta stop this. I'll drive myself nuts. For starters,

I better figure out where I'm headed and when I can safely row back to the wharf.

I scrub at my face and sit up straight. The mist flutters and twists in the wind. There's no one on the stern thwart.

A bigger wave sloshes to starboard. Quickly I unship the oars. Battling three more big waves, I keep rowing. What's going on? The cove's one of the most sheltered the length of the shore.

Then terror cuts off my breathing, as sudden as if Mel's fingers were squeezing my throat. Somehow, in the mist, I've rowed all the way to the entrance of the cove where the waves come in from the open ocean. I can hear them breaking against the rocks, the sound muted by the fog. *Boom...splash.*

If I stray outside the cove, I'll be on the rocks before I know it. Knucklebones and Hare's Ears are west of here, Hook Nose to the east. High tide or not, it's no place for a dory, especially with me at the oars; I don't have the strength to keep myself clear of those reefs.

Watching the waves, choosing my timing, I turn the dory 180 degrees, and take big, steady sweeps with the oars. But the wind's against me, and the tide's turned, running fast now. The horrible *whomp* of the waves grows louder. My breath's raw in my throat as I heave it in, gasp it out. My ribs hurt, pain jabbing my side; each arm is one big ache from wrist to shoulder. I'm praying again, little scraps of prayer that don't make sense.

Maybe I'm being punished for my sins. In desperation, I try to picture the Virgin Mary in her blue dress at the stern—the same place where Janie was, only a few minutes ago.

The rocks *are* closer. As the mist shifts, briefly I catch sight of their wet, black bulk. In sheer panic I drag on the oars, knives stabbing my shoulders and wrists.

Prinny...

A voice out of the mist, faint and wispy. A quiver of hope travels the length of my spine. Janie's voice, I'm sure it's hers. She knows how quick I could crash into the rocks. She knows waves could swamp the dory—that I could drown in the ice-cold water right here at the entrance to Fiddlers Cove.

Alls I have to do is follow her voice.

Strength pours into me. I put my back into my strokes, row as I've never rowed in my life before, and the only thing I can think about is how full my days are now. There's Ma, doing her best to get her act together. Da, who's making me a headboard. Tansy and Rogue. Travis, my very first friend. My new girlfriend Laice. LaVaughn, who's sometimes as real to me as Travis and Laice. Hector, who sits with me in the canteen; Rayleen and her recipes; the foxes in their den. Even Mrs. Dooks, who thought my reading was excellent.

Prinny...

TWENTY-SIX

true con·fes′sions

"...*Prinny*."

Janie's voice cuts through the slaps and slops of the sea, overrides a distant roaring like a rogue wave slamming into the rocks. She's guiding me into the cove, encouraging me the only way she can. Again, hope puts meat on my muscles; the dory ploughs up one side of a wave and down the other.

"Prinny!"

I know *that* voice. I'd know it anywhere.

"Da!" I shout. "I'm over here!"

One of the oars skips over the crest of the swell, slicing through empty air. The dory skews, broadside to the waves. With the last of my strength, I bring her around.

Da shouts a second time, a shout as loud as any foghorn. The roaring's louder, too. I dart a look over my shoulder; the bow of *Wilma Marie*, white and solid, is the most beautiful sight in the whole world.

I scream, "Don't come too close to the rocks!"

Da's standing up in his yellow oilskins, peering

through the fog. I didn't need to warn him. If there's anyone knows the cove, the rocks, the reefs and currents of these waters, it's Da.

I keep rowing. *Wilma Marie* edges closer.

"Hold her steady and grab the buoy when I throw it," Da says, calm as if we're at a Sunday picnic. "Wilma, you take the tiller."

He's talking to Ma. *Ma.* Out in a boat, close to the rocks, sitting on the rear thwart and clutching the tiller like it's the only solid thing for miles.

Da picks up a coil of rope attached to a bright orange buoy, swings the buoy, and with one heave tosses it toward me. It thunks against the thwart, right at my feet. Quickly I ship the oars and seize the buoy, hugging it to my chest.

The rope goes taut. The gap between the dory and *Wilma Marie* narrows. Wood bumps against fiberglass, then Da's big hand reaches down and holds the dory firm. "Climb aboard," he says. "You're doing good."

First though, I stretch for the hawser and toss it to him. No sense losing a good dory. By the time I get my feet under me, Da's jammed one boot on top of the hawser. His free hand wraps around mine and I tumble aboard, my knees scraping the gunwale, my cold fingers grasping center-thwart as hard as Ma's are grasping the tiller. Da tosses the buoy in the bilge. Then he picks up the hawser, crosses to stern, and ties it fast.

"Okay, Wilma," he says, "I'll take over."

"You mean I gotta let go?"

"You're safe with me," Da says patiently; I figure it isn't the first time he's said it. She slides along the thwart to give him room, her knuckles in a death-grip on the edge. Da takes the tiller, goes into reverse, then jacks up the power. As we turn in a big circle, sending up a curving wave of white, Ma cringes and the rocks disappear into the fog.

I start to tremble.

Ma lets go of the thwart. She hauls air into her lungs. Keeping low, looking straight ahead rather than at the water all around us, she scrambles toward me. I'm not just trembling now. I'm shaking and I can't stop. Ma puts her arms around me and holds me.

"Prinny," she whispers. "Oh, Prinny, we were so scared. We couldn't find you in the fog, we couldn't find you anywheres, and I could see Tom was worried sick. I kept calling your name, over and over…"

Her hair's wet from the mist. Was it Ma I heard? Or Janie Elizabeth?

I'll never know the answer, and I'm not sure it matters.

"Prinny, I loves you so much," Ma says.

"I loves you too, Ma." I burrow my head in her shoulder, letting her comfort me. She rocks me back and forth, her cheek in my hair, her arms strong and sure.

Wilma Marie is making short work of the trip back to the wharf. Too short. I like being held by my ma, feeling she's stronger than me.

Da brings the boat into the wharf until we're nudging the pilings. After tying the hawser loose around the lowest metal rung, he kills the motor. Silence rings in my ears.

"Ma," I say, because I still can't quite believe it, "you came out in a boat?"

Her eyes flick from the water, which is still rocking from our wake, to the solid bulk of the wharf, and then to my face. "I did. Yeah, I did," she says as if she can't believe it herself. "I had to. I couldn't have stayed on shore with you lost in the fog and Tom out looking for you on his own—I'd have gone stark mad."

"That was right brave," I say. She blushes geranium-red, opens her mouth, shuts it, and grips my fingers so tight it's painful.

Then she says, looking over her shoulder, "Tom's the one who found you. Him on the water—I never understood before." Her eyes are filmed with tears. "I doubt there's a fisherman within a hundred miles could've rescued you as quick as Tom did."

Da's gazing at the bilge like it's heaped with gold doubloons. "We better get her home, Wilma. She's cold and wet. Sore arms too, I bet."

"Thanks, Da," I say huskily. "I was real scared out

there." I stand up, my knees quivering, clamber to the stern, and put my arms around him. He's too big for my hands to meet around his waist. I clutch him with all my strength, and that's when his arms come around me, slow at first, like he's testing the water, then more definite like he means it. We stand there for a long time.

Carefully Ma works her way to the stern. One arm around Da, one around me, she says, "This is alls we need."

Twenty minutes later, I'm in my pj's, sitting in the rocker with the mohair blanket around my legs and Tansy on my lap. Da's at the table, whittling on a piece of kindling. Ma's making hot chocolate, adding extra marshmallows until a thick white goop floats on top.

She says, "Kraft Dinner tonight, by the looks of it."

There's things I have to say before I lose my nerve. But first I ask, "How did you arrive at the cove so soon?"

"We got a phone call," Ma says. "From a girl who wouldn't give her name. She said you were lost in the fog in a dory and we should go and rescue you right away."

My jaw drops. Mel wouldn't have the smarts to warn anyone. Tate lacks the conscience. Sigrid. It must have been Sigrid. Knowing about boats, she'd have realized the danger I was in.

In a weird way, I suppose you could say she saved my life.

Heartbeat stammering in my ears, I say, "I got a confession to make."

Da grins, looking into every corner of the kitchen. "Don't see no sign of Father Gogan."

"I'm serious, Da." As Ma's eyes and mine lock into each other, my voice cracks open. "I'm the one who left the two bottles of rum in the back room for you to find, Ma. I'm sorry, I'm so sorry. I was that angry the day the cats got loose that I wanted you out of the house. Da, it was my fault Ma started drinking. All my fault!"

"Now, Prinny," Ma says, "wasn't you unscrewed the bottle and took the first gulp. Anyways, I could've gone to Baldwin's and bought my own booze."

"And it wasn't you who let the cats out, Ma. I thought it was, that day. But the next day, when I went back to school, I found out it was the Shrikes—the three girls who were blackmailing me. But I didn't tell you, I let you blame yourself. How come I was so mean?"

I'm crying by now. Ma says, still sounding like the strong one, "But I did leave the doors open that morning, for nearly an hour. The cats weren't on my radar, I was that frantic not to take a drink...don't fret yourself over it."

"I should've told the truth."

"So you're not perfect. A regular mix-up of good and bad, same as the rest of us."

"I went to the wharf this afternoon to tell Da. I had to tell someone, it was sitting on me heavy as those rocks."

"One thing to look for me at the wharf," Da says. "Another to head out in a dory in a pea-souper with the tide turning."

"The same three girls were down there. They were chasing me—that's why I took to the dory."

Da seems to grow taller as I watch. "Three girls ganged up on you? Then left you out there in the fog?"

"But one of them phoned," I say. "It must have been Sigrid."

Da says in a quiet voice that means business, "Phone call or no phone call, I'll be after visiting all their parents. The school, too. You could've drowned, Prinny."

"Da, you don't like going anywhere near the school."

"I never was much for school, you're right about that. All them desks anchored to the floor, going no place fast. But my dander's up—the principal's going to get an earful."

Da protecting me. That's a new one.

Even though the hot chocolate's still hot, my fingers feel like frozen fish sticks. "I'm not finished," I say. "The day I got my monthlies, I went looking for pads in your drawer, Ma. I found out about Janie Elizabeth."

Da's knife clatters on the table. Ma stands with her mouth open, a saucepan in one hand, the salt cellar in the other. She's gone pale.

Frightened, I say, "I shouldn't have said anything! But you never told me I had a sister, you kept her a secret like you'd forgotten her and—"

"I've never forgotten her," Ma says.

"Is she why you took to drink?"

Carefully she puts the saucepan on the stove. "Janie wasn't the reason—although she was the excuse I gave myself. I drank because of my dad. Along with Ida being so mean, Bethana going out west, me feeling trapped in Ratchet—"

"Trapped because I didn't die? Like Janie?"

"I never wanted you dead!"

"But you had to get married because you were pregnant. So you *were* trapped."

Da's digging the point of his knife into the kindling. Ma says with some of her old spirit, "We weren't the first ones to make a rush trip to the priest, and we won't be the last." She tosses salt into the saucepan, a little smile playing around her lips. "Tom was so good to me, so respectful of my feelings, and we were young…one thing led to another. Not that I recall Tom objecting."

"Now, Wilma," Da says, and if a man can look horrified and pleased as punch all at once, he's managing.

Ma puts the saucepan down on the stove. "Wasn't in my plans to get pregnant right away, Prinny. When we found out it was twins, two for the price of one, it was a shocker. But we picked out names, and your Da made two cradles out of pine, smooth and sweet-smelling as could be."

"Why did you call me Prinny?"

"My first dory," Da says, "when I was a tyke. Called *Primula*, she was, because my ma loved flowers. I couldn't get my tongue around *Primula*, so I named her *Prinny*. Handled like a dream, that little dory."

A boy with a shock of brown hair tugging his dory along the shore, trousers wet to the knee…

"Prinny," I breathe. "It's a lovely name."

"Janie was born with the cord tight around her neck," Ma says softly. "Nothing anyone could do. Near to broke my heart. And Tom's."

Her fingers are still curled around the salt cellar. "That's when I started making stuff. Potholders, candles, stupid-looking seagulls, you name it—anything to keep busy. And every now and then, when you were having a nap and the house was quiet, I'd pour myself a nice drink of rum." Her sigh comes from her toes. "Never thought there was no harm in it."

"I always thought your drinking was my fault, Ma. I tried so hard to be good, so I wouldn't set you off."

"It was never your fault. Never. Not yours, not your Da's." She takes a deep breath. "Now that I've gone once to AA, I'll go every week." She gulps more air. "There's a couple jobs opening up at Tim Hortons. I'm thinking of applying. I needs to be around people, I figured that out in the taverns and clubs. So I talked to the manager, told her straight up about the drinking and how I was taking them pills, and she told me to put in my application."

"Well now," says Da, his face squinched up.

I say, "Days you work, I can make supper."

"You wouldn't mind?"

"I like cooking." I wink at Da. "Maybe I'll get a raise."

"Tom?" Ma says, and I can see she's afraid of what he might say.

"You do what's best for you, Wilma. If you're happy, I'm happy." He gives me his slow smile. "I'm in hopes Prinny will be happy, too."

Right there in the kitchen, it's like there's a rope connecting the three of us, so tight it's singing.

Twenty-seven

'roll·er 'coast·er

I wake up next morning in planning mode.

(1) Tell Travis about Janie Elizabeth and how hateful I was to Ma. I might even tell him how I let Tate blackmail me.

(2) Ditto Laice.

In less than a month Laice will be gone from here, back to her mother or her father. Back—I truly hope—to living with her sister. And I'll be back to square one. Missing her something fierce, and with no girlfriend.

(3) Make friends with Hud. Him and his little sister Fleur. Will Travis be okay with that? Will I ever understand why I have to do it?

(4) Come up with some short lines in honor of my twin sister Janie Elizabeth. Call those short lines by their proper name. A poem.

(5) Write down my poems.

(6) Keep reading. Short lines and longer ones.

(7) Take control of the roller coaster.

I'm on it again, that's easy to see; somehow Ma

going out in the boat made the slope steeper. Last night was grand—Da, Ma, and me. But I don't know what'll happen when Father Gogan comes for a visit, or Aunt Ida. Or if a customer's rude to Ma at Tim Hortons. Captain Morgan's been a friend of hers for a long time.

I could stick a happy face on my calendar for each day Ma stays sober. Who knows, maybe I'll end up with a string of happy faces, a necklace that'll loop around the whole house.

(8) Never hide booze in the closet again. What I'm trying to say is, be a good daughter.

(9) Leave *perfect* to Ben the dog.

I head for the porch to make a start on (2). As I'm putting on my jacket, which is a struggle because my arms are real sore, someone knocks on the door.

Laice is standing outside. Her face is one big smile. "I'm so glad you're safe! You were really brave, out in a little boat in the fog. You have to tell me all about it."

"I was coming over—"

"This summer, will you teach me how to row?"

"But…you'll be gone by then."

She tugs a letter from her pocket and waves it in my face. "From Mum. The court hearing's been delayed until fall. So she's asking if I want to stay in Ratchet for the summer."

I suck in my breath. "Do you want to?"

"Of course I do! Now that I'm used to it, I really like it here. And guess what? My Hadden grandparents want to go to Alberta in July—so my sister Lynette will come here for three weeks. You'll get to meet her."

"We could all go to the fox den. The pups will be big by then."

"You and I can read together every day."

We're smiling at each other like a couple of fools. Three whole months! We'll get to be even better friends, I know we will. Which is when I understand that if you love someone, you're always on a roller coaster.

I never stopped loving Ma.

It'll be like losing a sister when Laice leaves.

I'm going along for the ride anyway.

Jill MacLean's writing has always drawn on experiences in her life. Her books are set in Newfoundland, where her son and his family now live. Over the years, she's canoed, kayaked, hiked, and snowmobiled there, travelled the coves by boat, and stayed in the outports. Little did Jill realize at the time that these experiences could all be called "research," or that her love of the province would translate into words. Jill lives in Bedford, Nova Scotia.